GIRL V THE WORLD

Invisible Me

hardie grant EGMONT

Invisible Me
published in 2013 by
Hardie Grant Egmont
Ground Floor, Building 1, 658 Church Street
Richmond, Victoria 3121, Australia
www.hardiegrantegmont.com.au

A CiP record for this title is available from the National Library of Australia

Text copyright © 2013 Chrissie Keighery
Illustration and design copyright © 2013 Hardie Grant Egmont

Design by Michelle Mackintosh
Cover photograph by Sharon Heiz
Text design and typesetting by Ektavo

Printed in Australia by Griffin Press, an Accredited ISO AS/NZS
14001:2004 Environmental Management System printer.

1 3 5 7 9 10 8 6 4 2

FSC
www.fsc.org
MIX
Paper from
responsible sources
FSC® C009448

The paper this book is printed on is certified against the
Forest Stewardship Council® Standards. Griffin Press holds
FSC chain of custody certification SGS-COC-005088. FSC
promotes environmentally responsible, socially beneficial
and economically viable management of the world's forests.

Chrissie Keighery

hardie grant EGMONT

'Sunday roast,' Dad says. 'That smells good, Vanny.'

I look up from my school books on the kitchen table. Dad is standing behind Mum at the oven, wrapping his arms around her waist as she checks the roast inside.

'Ew ... get a room guys,' I tease. But, inside, I feel my heart skip. It's so nice to have Dad back. In the two weeks he was gone, staying with his sister, Kate, there was sort of a hole in my heart.

'Cheeky,' Dad says, smiling at me over his shoulder and looking back. 'Vanny, I think we have us a teenager on our hands.'

Cricket barks her agreement from the doorway in our hall. We got her from the pound – she's a rescue dog and we're the rescuers. I still can't imagine why anyone would have wanted to get rid of her. Mum says some people like the idea of having a puppy, but when the puppy grows up they're not so keen anymore. But I reckon she's as cute as any puppy. Apparently, she was found wandering around without a collar, so no-one knew her name. But as soon as I saw Cricket, I knew what I wanted to call her. She jumped up to say hello. Like a little cricket.

Even though we only got her a few months ago, it's as though she's been with me forever. In a way, Cricket is like the sister I used to wish for before I totally gave up hope that my parents would have another child. And Cricket has something to say about everything.

I give Dad one of my best eye rolls. 'I've been a teenager for three months, Dad,' I remind him.

'Good,' Dad says. 'Only six years and nine months to go.' He starts moving towards me, his fingers twitching. The next thing I know, I'm out of my seat and enduring a tickle. Cricket jumps around beside and between us, trying to be part of the action.

'Dad, I'm too … old … for this,' I gasp, and I try to be serious so he'll get it, but I can't help giggling. Cricket barks again, six short barks that seem to echo my words.

'Ssssh, Cricket,' Dad says, releasing me. 'Now sit.'

Cricket stops barking and sits still. I can see that the sitting is killing her. She's definitely a jumper by nature, not a sitter. Three seconds later, she's up and racing down the hallway, as if those three seconds have given her super-energy savings that she has to use up somehow.

'How long before it's ready, Vanny?' Dad asks.

'You've got time to watch the news,' Mum answers. Dad nods, grabs the local paper and goes into the lounge room.

'Hey, Limps,' Mum says when he's gone, 'can you come and help me choose an outfit for my party while we're waiting?'

Mum's birthday is in a couple of weeks and she's having some friends over. I'm supposed to be doing my maths homework, but I guess I can do it after dinner.

Maybe it's lame, but I love choosing outfits with Mum.

I like the way she wants my opinion on things and I like that it's girly time. But I especially like having this girly time with Mum while Dad is watching the news in the lounge room, while he's home and settled and it seems like he's happy.

V

As Mum is looking through her wardrobe, I sneak a look in Dad's dresser drawer. Everything that should be there is. His wallet and keys are perched on top of a stack of his undies. It's a nice feeling. I slide the drawer shut quietly before Mum turns around.

'Okay, Limps, these are our options.' Mum holds her favourite little black dress up in front of her, and then switches to her red polka-dot shirt and black pants. Even though she's wearing Vans, she manages to squish her feet halfway into her high-heeled black wedges and teeter towards me.

'I reckon the little black dress,' I say, lying back on their bed. 'Except that it's just a bit too plain.'

Mum screws up her nose. 'You're right,' she says. 'Can I

try your short-sleeve cardigan over the top? The red one?'

Now it's my turn to screw up my nose. 'Mum, you'll stretch it!' I protest.

Mum gives me one of her grins. 'Limps, that might have been true six months ago, but not anymore. Some things have changed lately. Two things, actually.'

I look down at my chest. She's right. I'm definitely catching up to her in that way.

Mum comes over. She sits on the bed and bumps me so I'll make room for her.

'I reckon you're going to take after Dad's side of the family,' she giggles.

'Like Aunty Kate? No way!' I say, but I can't help laughing too. Aunty Kate's boobs are ginormous. It's so weird to think that I might get bigger boobs than my mum has. I mean, Mum is pretty flat for a grown-up, and I wouldn't mind being a bit bigger than she is eventually. But I definitely don't want *ginormous.*

'Maybe halfway between me and Aunty Kate?' Mum asks, and it's as though we're making a bargain and I get to choose exactly how I want to turn out in the end.

Of course, you don't actually get to choose how you turn out. If you did, I'd put in plenty of orders, starting with the gap in my teeth closing and going right down to my legs turning browner and being less skinny. I *wish* that was possible.

'Halfway and absolutely no more than that,' I offer.

'Done!' Mum says. 'Now can you get the cardie for me to try?'

I'm setting the table for dinner when Dad comes in from the lounge room.

'Did you know your friend was in this?' he asks, handing me the local paper. 'The pretty, dark-haired one.' I know straight away who Dad is referring to, because this is the sort of description people use about my best friend, Edi. *Pretty. Beautiful. Stunning. Attractive.* That's Edi. Edi hasn't mentioned anything about being in the local paper, though.

Dad has flipped it to a page near the back. It's a regular

feature in the paper. A photographer just goes around our local shopping centre, taking random pictures of people who look good. Usually, the people photographed are much older than me and Edi, but there she is. She's looking just her normal amount of gorgeous. If they'd taken a photo of me (which they totally wouldn't because I just don't stand out from the crowd), I'd probably have red eyes, or my hair sticking up, or my stomach sticking out, or I'd be opening my mouth so my gappy teeth would be showing. Or, most likely, all of the above. I feel a rush of pride that this girl is my absolute best friend.

SUNDAY STYLE SNAPSHOT

Edi Rhineheart
Who are you shopping with today? *My friend, Hazel.*
What are you looking for? *A necklace or something for my hair. I'll know when I see it.*
What are you wearing? *My fave old yellow T-shirt with sparkles, G-Star jeans and some cowboy boots I found at a market.*

I stare at the paper. The only line I see at the moment is the first one.

Who are you shopping with today? *My friend, Hazel.*

I look at the date on the cover of the paper. The photo would have been taken last Sunday. A week ago.

Last Sunday, I was home all day. By myself. No-one called at all.

Something flutters inside me.

Hazel has definitely been spending more and more time with Edi, but I think – I *hope* – that's because their boyfriends are mates. None of the boys at school like me, even though when some guys posted up a 'hot list' of all the girls in our year, I was actually ranked way higher than Hazel. We ripped up the list, but I still know everyone's positions. I was number eight and Hazel ended up being number twenty-three. Of course, Edi was number one.

I guess they could have been shopping, all four of them, but I doubt it. I don't think you'd get Edi's boyfriend, Archie, near shops on the weekend, since he's always playing soccer.

'She looks good, doesn't she, Olympia?' Dad says.

He lifts his arm in the air, fingers out and I'm already annoyed by what he's about to do, but here it comes anyway. 'Yo,' he says, moving his hand around like he *thinks* rappers do, 'girl got style.'

Yeah, Edi's got style. And she's also got Hazel, sticking to her like glue. Going shopping with her when it should have been me. And neither of them has even mentioned it to me all week.

I flick Dad's hand away and finish setting the table in silence.

'Here we go,' Mum says, putting plates on the table. 'Lamb roast.'

I probably could have figured that out by myself, since I'm seeing it with my own eyes.

Dad gets a cold beer from the fridge and hoes in immediately, like he's starving.

'So good, Vanny,' he says between mouthfuls.

Mum smiles at him, loads up her fork and has a taste. I push the food around on my plate, about as unhungry as I can get after seeing that article. Cricket positions herself under the table. I sneak her a piece of meat.

'So, what's on tomorrow, Limps?' Mum asks. 'Do you have sport? I've got your PE uniform washed and ready to go. It's on the bench in the laundry.'

'I've got PE second period,' I say. 'Softball.' *With Edi and Hazel. Who went shopping together and didn't even tell me.*

'Your dad was really good at softball,' Mum says, giving Dad one of her flirty looks. Mum and Dad started going out together when they were still in high school, so they know this random stuff about each other. They had me when they were both nineteen. I wasn't exactly *planned.*

Dad shakes his head, but I can tell he's pleased. Like, even though that was about a hundred years ago.

'Your mum was more of a netball fiend,' Dad says, as though the subject is interesting for me. 'She was a very cool centre. All over the court.'

'Great,' I say. Since I'm bad at sports, I don't know what all this has to do with me. I try to pull myself up. That was too sarcastic. I should have just gone along with them. 'At least softball is better than aths,' I add, to soften my 'great'. As I say it, I sneak another piece of meat down to Cricket.

'Olympia,' Dad says, 'are you feeding Cricket at the table?'

As soon as she hears her name, Cricket emerges from under the table and tries to jump on my lap.

'Down!' Dad says. He takes Cricket by the collar and walks her over to the side of the kitchen.

'Sit. Stay,' he says, and then returns to his chair. 'Olympia, Cricket obviously didn't get much training at her last home, so it's up to us to teach her how to behave. If you feed her at the table, you're letting her think she's human and equal. She needs to learn her place in the family.'

He turns to Cricket again. She's up and about to head back to me.

'Sit. Stay,' Dad says, his index finger pointing at her. Cricket does it, but she doesn't look happy. She lies down and tilts her head to the side.

'Aw, look at her. She's so cute,' Mum says.

I *am* looking at her and she *is* so cute. But Dad shakes his head.

'Naughty isn't cute,' he says. 'If you let her jump all over you, she will think it's okay to go jumping all over guests too. And I can tell you, a lot of people would find that anything *but* cute. What she needs is to go to obedience school.'

I feel my shoulders tense up. It was the whole obedience school idea that caused things to crash around here last time, when Dad ended up moving in with Aunty Kate. Dad wanted Cricket to start straight away, but the conversation about dog training somehow morphed into an argument about stuff that has nothing to do with Cricket.

I guess it's kind of normal to have parents who don't agree about everything. But I don't think most parents argue like mine. If they have an argument about one thing, it turns into an argument about five million things all mushed in together, and they just kept going on and on and getting louder and louder. I don't think that's normal.

I watch Mum take another bite of her dinner and chew silently. It's been so good between them tonight. But now I have that horrible, familiar feeling that things are about to change.

'Actually, Jim, you were going to do obedience school with Olympia, remember?'

The tension spreads from my shoulders all the way through me.

'Well, I can't do it now. I don't have time since I've got three new contracts in the pipeline.' He pauses. My leg jiggles up and down, bumping the table. 'Contracts I tendered for because you said we didn't have enough money, Savannah,' he adds.

I switch legs. I can see the water in the jug on the table going up and down with the jiggle. Nobody notices.

'*I* never said we didn't have enough money,' Mum says. She points to the fridge, where loads of bills are put up with magnets. 'The bills on the fridge said that. And if you *care* to remember, I've also taken an extra shift at work.'

'Come on, Savannah,' Dad says. 'You're home by four on Thursdays. Do it then.'

'Well, yes, Jim, why not?' Mum says and now her voice is kind of high-pitched. I can't really blame Cricket for barking because it's probably hurting her sensitive ears. 'As long as everyone's happy not to have the laundry and the shopping and cleaning and cooking done.'

Now I'm totally wishing that I didn't freak out after seeing the article and picture of Edi, because *something* started changing the mood in our kitchen and it was probably me. I can't remember how this argument even began, but if I'd just acted interested in Dad being good at softball a hundred years ago and Mum being centre in netball, maybe none of this would be happening.

I don't care if Mum never does another load of laundry or cooks another meal. I would eat baked beans every night and wear dirty clothes if I could stop this. But they're firing words at each other and there's nothing I can do.

'God, you're such a *matyr*, Savannah,' Dad says sarcastically. Mr Mendes just taught us that word in English. *Somebody who makes sacrifices or suffers greatly in order to advance a cause or principle.* Mum is not going to like being called that.

'Oh, do us all a favour and *grow up*, Jim,' she hisses.

I wish they'd look at me. If they did, they could *see* how sad it makes me when they fight.

I ease myself out of my seat carefully, but it wouldn't really matter if I did it like an elephant. Because Mum and Dad don't even notice I exist at the moment. I'm invisible.

When I close the door to my bedroom, I can still hear Mum and Dad arguing but I can't hear what they're saying.

I get my pyjamas on, turn the volume up on the TV and grab my drawing pad. Cricket jumps in bed beside me and burrows under the doona with her head sticking out. I give her a scratch between the ears.

After a while, Mum comes in. She sits on the end of my bed and sighs. With my bedroom door open, I can hear Dad turning on the TV in the spare room.

'Can you believe your father, Olympia?' Mum sighs. It's not a question she wants me to answer. I know all about this. Mum just wants to let off steam.

'Sometimes I wonder about him,' she says. 'For starters, did you see how many beers he had tonight? Did you count them, Limps?'

I shake my head. I don't even *want* to count how many beers Dad had.

'Well, he had five,' Mum continues. 'And five beers means he's gone stupid.'

Cricket burrows further down the doona. I wish I could do the same.

'I know he was young when you came along, but so was I.' Now I'm hoping Mum doesn't say anything about me being a surprise. Even though she always says I was a *good surprise,* sometimes I wish I didn't even know. Sometimes, it makes me feel like I was an *accident* instead of a surprise.

Mum lies on the end of my bed, propped up on an elbow, like she's making herself comfortable for a long session. I wriggle my legs under the covers so she has less room, but she just shifts around them.

'He just needs to step up to the plate. It's like, *Hello, Jim!* You have a family.'

Thankfully, at least Mum skips the part about me being a surprise this time.

'And a mortgage. So just get over yourself and stop –'

'Mum,' I say. 'I'm really tired.' If I have to hear any more, I think I'll scream.

Mum looks at me and then at her watch. As though I must be saying I'm tired because it's after my normal bedtime, not because I don't want to have this conversation.

'Oh, okay, Limps. You sleep tight. Don't worry about any of this.'

Yeah, right.

I settle back down in bed and pick up my drawing. I've been working on it for a while now. It's the four of us – Edi, Hazel, Jess and me – lounging around Edi's caravan. It's not from a photo or even my memory, just how I think the four of us might look when we're deep in conversation at one of our caravan meetings.

We're on the little lime-green bench seats and I'm sitting right next to Edi, where I'm *supposed* to sit, though sometimes Hazel is really annoying and gets in there before me. Hazel and Jess are opposite.

I add a few strokes with my lead pencil, but my heart's not in it tonight. I might be sitting next to Edi in the picture, but she and Hazel have gone shopping together in real life, and they didn't even ask me.

It makes me feel like I don't matter, all over again. Like I'm just as invisible to my friends as I am to my parents.

Cricket puts her little head over the page.

'You know what?' I whisper. She pricks up her ears. 'I'm glad you don't just sit and stay.'

Cricket looks up as though she's waiting for me to explain what I mean. I can hear Dad closing the door of the spare room and then getting into the wonky single bed in there that squeaks. At least he hasn't gone to Aunty Kate's.

I look up at the picture above my bed. It's a heart-shaped cloud, floating through a blue sky. Edi has the pair. Her cloud is floating in the opposite direction. We bought them at the op shop together. And it's right that Edi has one and I have the other, because *we* are a pair. We've just drifted a little bit.

'If you just sit and stay,' I say to Cricket, 'then you're just hanging around. Stuff happens, and you just let it happen.' *Like Hazel getting closer to Edi and pushing me out,* I think.

I give Cricket a scratch between the ears.

But I'm going to make sure that doesn't happen. All I have to do is figure out how to be a little more exciting than Hazel. Then things will go back to how they should be.

Even if I don't know how just yet.

Two

When I get up the next morning, Mum and Dad have both gone to work. The dirty dishes from last night's dinner are still in the sink. Messy. Like our family.

When I get to school, everyone's trying to push to their lockers at the same time as usual. Ella Ingram's locker is next to mine. She's had her hair cut so it's all short and spiky. It's a bit of a shock. Ella Ingram was number four on the hot list. It seems pretty risky to go that short. I guess it suits her, in a way, but I *so* wouldn't do something like that.

'Ella!' Edi saunters up to the locker area like she's got

heaps of time, but she actually doesn't because the bell has already gone.

'Oh my god, your hair looks amazing! Where did you get it done?'

Ella touches her spikes. 'Fur,' she says. 'Do you really like it?'

'I really do,' Edi says, and Edi doesn't say stuff she doesn't mean. 'It's so indie. *Everybody's* got long hair, and it's sooo boring.' She turns to me. 'What do you think, Limps?'

Actually, Edi has a point. I can't help touching my own hair. Maybe it's time *I* got a proper haircut? Mine isn't really in a style like Ella's. It's just kind of long and it's probably exactly the type of boring that Edi's talking about. But then again, I don't think a short style would suit me. It would probably draw too much attention to my gappy teeth.

'It's really nice, Ella,' I offer.

Ella just nods. She barely even glances at me. I can tell she's stoked that Edi likes her haircut. Everybody wants to impress Edi. But it's really rude that Ella directs everything to her and nothing to me. 'I had to save up for ages to go to that salon, but –'

'Edi,' I say, 'we'd better get going.' It's bad enough that I haven't done my homework. I don't want to be late too.

When we get to class, Edi heads down to the front of the room with the other brainiacs who are way ahead of us. I have just enough time to slide into my regular seat at the table with Hazel and Jess before Mr Cartwright arrives. He's carrying a huge mug of steaming coffee. He does that all the time. I reckon he's rubbing it in that he's the teacher so he's allowed to drink coffee during class.

He walks around the classroom, coffee in one hand and the other outstretched to collect our homework. Nick Bradbury shadows him. You're not even allowed to talk in Mr C's class, let alone get up and walk around. Nick gets away with a lot because of his Down syndrome. It *is* kind of unfair, but nobody seems to mind so I try not to as well. Besides, it is pretty funny – every time Mr C stops in front of someone and holds out his hand, Nick stops too. By the time Mr C and Nick get to my table, I'm smiling.

'I gather you're very happy because you've done a great job on your homework, Olympia?' he says.

I gulp as Hazel and Jess hand in their worksheets.

'Um ... I ... I didn't do it,' I say softly.

Mr C raises his big woolly eyebrows and makes me wait for his response. Nick stands behind him.

'So, let me guess, O-lym-pia.' He stretches out the syllables. 'Typhoid? Cholera? The Bubonic Plague? These would be examples of valid excuses for the incompletion of a task set two weeks ago.'

He pauses again. Some people twitter and I know they think Mr C is pretty funny when he says stuff like that. But right now, I can feel the eyes of the entire class on me and it doesn't feel funny at all.

I feel like my life is one big, gigantic stress. I wish I could swap lives with someone – preferably with Edi, who is looking at me from her advanced-maths table, with her homework completed in front of her, and her wardrobe of great clothes and parents who don't fight at home. But I'd settle for being Hazel or even Jess.

Tears spring up from behind my eyes. I close them.

Then I hear Nick's voice. 'Don't make Olympia sad, Mr C.'

It sort of shifts my feelings about Nick. It's sweet, the

way he's sticking up for me. Nick is the only one who would even try to get away with talking to Mr C like that, and it's pretty brave that he does it. But it does double the tears, because he's right. I *am* sad and it's *so* not even about my maths homework. I feel a tear dribble down my cheek, even though my eyes are still shut. When I open them, Mr Cartwright has put down his coffee. He goes to touch my shoulder, but then probably thinks better of it since teachers aren't supposed to touch students.

'I have stuff going on at home,' I mumble. Even though my words come out really small, I can tell everyone's heard them. Hazel and Jess move their chairs closer to me, like human shields. Without me even telling them, they get that something would have happened with my parents. They've been through stuff like this with me before.

Mr C takes a breath. 'Okay. Don't worry about your homework, Olympia,' he says. 'You take as much time as you need.' Then he turns and points around the classroom. 'The rest of you,' he says, 'get on with it.'

I think it might be the first time in history that Mr C has publicly let someone off for not doing homework. Part of me is pleased I got away with it, now that my tears have dried up. If I ever have to hand it in, I'll just get the answers from a friend.

After maths, the girls all want to know what's going on at home, but we don't have much time between periods so we can't chat properly. I mutter something about Mum and Dad, and they stick protectively close to me as we head over to the gym.

Miss Kearns is standing at the front of the gym. She lifts her whistle and blows really hard.

'All right, people,' she yells. 'Change of plans. Softball field's being used by another class. Running races instead. Into your regular groups and on the oval. Now.'

Miss Kearns talks like she's running. Like she's in too much of a hurry to use full sentences, and we should be too.

I groan. Running sucks, but my running group sucks more. Since we go in order of birthdates, I'm always stuck in Leni's group. Leni is ridiculous. She's tall and super athletic-looking. But her legs are so muscly they make her look really boyish. She doesn't really seem to care about that, though. She's more into winning races than looking right and, believe me, she does that. *Every time.* If I was her, I'd try to cut down on the training and get rid of some of the muscles. I mean, I know my legs aren't great either. That's part of the reason I hate PE so much – the shorts we have to wear make my legs look even whiter and skinnier than normal.

I'm so not up for running today. But Miss Kearns is a hard-arse. She doesn't let anyone get out of PE unless they have a doctor's certificate or something.

When people start moving, I stay put. Hazel, Jess and Edi stay put with me. We all sit on the floorboards.

Miss Kearns starts to jog over to us, but she's intercepted by Anya. I can't hear what Anya is saying, but I can tell she's trying to get out of doing the running session. She's pointing to her feet, and I can see she's wearing school shoes and figure she's probably forgotten her runners accidentally-on-purpose. That's not good enough for Miss Kearns, though. She points the way to the oval. Anya shakes her head, but she goes.

Miss Kearns jogs up to us. 'What's the delay, girls?' she demands.

Edi puts her arms around me and gives me a squeeze. She looks at me, her big brown eyes asking for permission to talk. I nod.

'Miss, Olympia is having problems. At home.' Edi says it really quietly. For some reason, that makes it come out more serious.

Miss Kearns points towards the oval, but it's not with her arm stretched right out. It's more half-hearted than that.

I close my eyes for a moment and focus on how sad I was last night. It's not that hard to make a few tears come again. I amp up the feeling by thinking about how Edi and the girls are really trying to take care of me.

'*Emotional* problems,' Edi adds.

Miss Kearns looks at me. I'm guessing what she sees is pretty convincing. She starts backing away. What Edi has said, combined with my expression, seems to have affected her like kryptonite affects Superman.

'I'm very sorry about that, Olympia,' she says. 'You can sit this out. Just be a spectator.' And then, amazingly, she asks, 'Do you need a friend to stay with you?'

'Yes, please,' I say, my lips wobbling.

'*One* friend,' Miss Kearns calls, then she walks away.

I lean into Edi. 'Thanks anyway, Hazel and Jess.'

'Let's go, girls!' Miss Kearns yells.

Jess shrugs and gets up like it's no big deal, but Hazel gives me a weird look. It's kind of half-concerned and half-hurt she's being left out. I smile a wobbly smile back.

But, to be honest, this couldn't have worked out better.

Edi and I are the only ones sitting on the benches next to the oval as the others run, walk and limp around, depending on how keen they are. Leni's probably broken a few world records and is making everyone else look like they're running through quicksand. There's just the right amount of sun for sitting here – but way too much for running in the heat.

Hazel comes last in her race by ages. When she finally reaches the finish line, she turns and gives us a wave. Then she mouths something that's impossible to understand from here. It's annoying that she doesn't just let me and Edi be.

Edi waves to Hazel and does the thumbs-up sign, then Hazel does it back to her, which is a bit stupid because it's like celebrating that Hazel came last. It's obviously something between the two of them that I don't know about.

'What's been happening at home, Limps?' Edi asks when Hazel finally disappears. 'Is it just the same stuff, or is it worse? You seem more upset this time.'

I bite my lip. Edi and the others know how Mum and Dad argue about stupid things and then the fights sort of spiral out of control. I've told them how Mum talks to me about Dad being irresponsible with money and how he drinks too much and stuff like that. I've told them that he gets back at Mum by leaving the house to go and stay with Aunty Kate.

I sigh. In fact, what happened last night was pretty run-of-the-mill. I'm not sure why I'm more upset this time. Maybe it's because all their arguments have built up, one on top of another, and now it's like there's this giant stack of them taking up too much room in my head.

But none of that is very interesting. And if I tell her what happened last night, everything will blow over. My friends will be sympathetic, but pretty soon they'll be thinking and talking about other things.

Edi rubs my back. She's taking my silence as evidence that I'm too upset to talk. So I run with that.

'I don't really want to talk about it at school,' I find myself saying. 'Because it's way worse than usual. It's … it's full-on terrible. I'll probably start bawling, and I don't want to do that at school, in front of everyone.' I'm not quite sure where the *full-on terrible* came from, but Edi's eyes are wide and I can tell she's wondering what the *full-on terrible* thing might be.

'Oh, Limps,' she says. 'What we need is an emergency caravan meeting, so we can *focus* and talk this through. I'll get the girls together. I'm pretty sure everyone can do tomorrow afternoon. Is that okay for you?'

It's pretty cool that Edi's calling for an emergency meeting. Normally, our caravan meetings are on Friday afternoon. And I haven't been the one in the spotlight at our caravan meetings for ages. It's all been about Hazel getting her period and Edi wanting to ask Archie to go out with her.

I nod. Edi gives me a quick shoulder squeeze.

I take a breath. 'Edi, I saw you in the local paper,' I say softly.

Edi rolls her beautiful brown eyes, like being photographed for *Sunday Style Snapshot* is no big deal, like it's kind of naff. That's very Edi. She just takes it for granted that people think she's pretty and cool. Well, they're just the facts, I suppose. She's not vain, though. More like *realistic*.

'Yeah, I was just walking around with Hazel when that guy came up and asked me all those lame questions,' she says.

That's also very Edi. Not realising that leaving me out of the shopping trip might have hurt my feelings.

I chew on my lip. 'So, you went shopping with Hazel?'

'Yeah. We were on Facebook and I told her I had to go and get cardboard for a project and she said she'd come along.'

'Oh. I didn't see that conversation,' I say.

'Yeah, I just messaged Hazel because I wanted to tell her something Archie told me about Leo ...' Edi pauses and looks at me and I can tell she's finally getting it.

'Aw, Limps,' she continues, 'I only kept it between us because it wouldn't be interesting to anyone else. It was just about how Archie's mum cooked dinner for Leo the other night and he ate so much he almost puked. Then we just ended up talking about my project and me needing to get some cardboard.' Edi pauses. 'Limps, it wasn't like this big, planned *expedition* or anything,' she says.

I let out a sigh. I'm kind of sick of hearing about Archie and Leo all the time, but I'd still prefer to be included in a boring conversation than totally left out.

'I suppose I'm just a bit sensitive at the moment,' I say. 'You know, cos of the stuff with my parents. It's just that … well … I was sort of stuck at home. By myself.'

Edi tilts her head to the side. 'Oh, Limps,' she says. 'I'll make sure you're included from now on. Okay?'

'Okay,' I say, and it comes out sounding a bit too bright so I try again.

'Okay.'

Three

I go to Digby's Art Supplies after school. I don't have any money, but I like looking at canvases and paints and stuff. I get my monthly pocket money on Friday, so I might even find something small I can buy. It's so nice in the store that I go there even when I won't have any money for ages. Being around all that arty stuff is somehow soothing.

There's a set of paintbrushes on sale that I'm thinking about getting. They look really good. I pick one up and brush it on my wrist. The bristles are just the right texture. Not too soft that I wouldn't be able to get definition, and not too rough either.

Because they're on sale, I might even be able to afford a new sketchpad too. I pick one up and run my fingers over the thick, creamy pages. Then I look towards the counter and I notice a guy buying something at the counter. My heart races a little bit. I can only see the back of him, but I know it's *him*. The cute guy I've seen here before. He looks about my age and he has sandy hair and he's wearing a Kilmore High blazer. You can't just go to Kilmore High like you can go to my school. You have to be really smart to get in.

Bronwyn, who owns the store, is behind the counter. I watch as she throws her head back and laughs as she rings up the sale. It makes me wonder what he's said to her, but I can't hear the actual words from here. Also, even though I'm trying, I can't see what he's buying. I'm curious, though.

As he walks from the counter to the door, I can see his face. Well, part of his face anyway, because his hair flops down on one side. Yep, it's definitely Cute Art-Store Boy. As he walks out the door, he opens the bag and rummages through it with his hand. I wonder if he's excited about what's inside. Or whether they're just things he *had* to get for a school project or something.

I think about asking Bronwyn what he bought, but I don't. That would probably seem weird. A bit stalker-ish even.

V

When I get home, Dad's in the kitchen. And he's doing the dishes!

'Hey, Olympia,' he says casually, like last night never happened. 'Do you know where this goes?' He holds up a grater. I put it away in the cupboard next to the sink. As we're tidying, Mum walks in. A smile spreads over her face when she sees us. Then, she actually starts *singing*.

No amount of poetry
Would mend this broken heart
But you can put the Hoover 'round
If you want to make a start.

Dad laughs. 'I'm not vacuuming,' he says. 'But what about the dishes, Vanny? Does that count?'

'Absolutely,' Mum says.

And just like that, their latest argument is over.

Go figure.

V

Mum and Dad are on the couch in our lounge room, and I'm on the recliner with Cricket at my feet. So far, we've watched the news, *7.30* and *Four Corners*. They're not exactly TV programs that I'm into, but I don't go into my room. When things are good and easy like they are tonight, I feel like I have to hang around and soak it up. In a way, it's like lying around in the sunshine when you know the weather forecast is for storms. I want to *bask* in it and keep the feeling in my bones, for when things aren't good and easy.

Dad lifts Mum's feet onto his lap and gives them a massage. Cricket rolls on her back and I massage her tummy with my foot.

'I googled obedience schools,' Dad says, still rubbing Mum's feet. 'There's a class on Thursdays at five.'

Mum pulls her feet away, but Dad pulls them back. 'I was just thinking, Vanny, I've got a meeting quite close to the obedience school on Thursday. It will take a while. But maybe I could drop Olympia and Cricket there, and you can pick them up?'

Dad looks over to me. 'I mean, it's not as if you need either of us to be with you the whole time, is it, Olympia? I'm sure you're quite capable of dealing with the class alone.'

It's *really* nice to hear him say that. 'That's fine with me,' I say.

Mum smiles. 'Well, look at us ... *compromising*,' she says. 'That suits me too. Let's lock it in.'

The clock on our mantelpiece tells me it's almost ten, which is supposed to be my bedtime. But I give it a shot.

'I've got another idea for a compromise,' I say.

Mum and Dad look at each other and then back at me. Both of them are shaking their heads and smiling. I feel like they're enjoying this night as much as I am – which could be a good sign for what I'm about to ask.

'Seeing as I'm old enough to take Cricket to obedience school on my own, how about I get to stay up to watch *Acacia Lane*?'

That's one of the good things about my mum – she sometimes lets me stay up watching late-night TV shows with her. Most of my friends have to go to bed way before ten on weeknights. There's no way any of them would be allowed to stay up for a show that doesn't start until after that. Even though I don't get to watch it that often, I can usually figure out what's happening on *Acacia Lane*.

Mum does her little snorty laugh. 'I'm not sure that's a *compromise*, Limps,' she says. 'More like a *manipulation*.'

But when Dad just shrugs and smiles, I know I've won.

V

'All right, girls,' Dad says, putting a bowl of popcorn on the coffee table and picking up his book. 'Enjoy your soapie. I'd have to say, I'd rather stick pins in my eyes …'

'Dad … *sshhh*,' I say.

The theme song to *Acacia Lane* is really heavy on the piano. There's a run-through of stuff that's happened previously. This episode centres on my fave character. Veronica is fifteen, and a student at Beverly Hills High.

She has *the* best clothes you could ever imagine. Even better than Edi's. She lives in a mansion with her parents, equipped with an indoor pool and spa, a gym and a maid who picks up after her.

Heaven.

I'm completely in love with the orange shortie jumpsuit she's wearing as she sweeps into the giant kitchen. The background music is bright and cheerful as she scans the huge marble bench. Right in front of her, there's a brand-new, hot-pink *credit card* wrapped in a white bow. Oh my god. If that was me, I'd go *off*. But Veronica is used to stuff like that. All she does is pick the card up, smile a small smile and take her phone out of her awesome white handbag to write a text.

Thnx daddy.

Next thing you know, you see Veronica heading out of Juicy Couture with about fifty million shopping bags. She looks pretty happy, like you would be if you had fifty million bags like that. But then, her face falls. The camera scans to a red sports car parked across the road.

Someone gets out of the passenger seat, and then the

driver gets out. The background music goes from fun and light to super intense. At first, you can only see their backs, but when they walk up to each other on the sidewalk it's clear who they are.

Veronica's father and her mother's best friend. And right there, out on the street, they actually hook up!

The camera scans back to Veronica as she drops her bags to the pavement. The theme music starts. Now we'll have to wait for ages to see what happens.

V

As I lie in bed, I replay that scene in my head. It was so … *dramatic.* I kind of wish life was that dramatic. I mean, seeing something like that would be hard, for sure. But at least there's a *real* reason why it's hard.

In a way, I wish I had something like that going on in my life, rather than the boring stuff about how Mum and Dad keep arguing about nothing. Something to tell my friends that's *huge*. Something that's *way* more interesting than boyfriends who eat too much, or any of the other things we talk about. Something to make them sit up and pay attention to me.

That's what I need for the caravan meeting tomorrow. Something *dramatic* to share.

Four

School is totally boringsville on Tuesday morning. Edi, Jess and Hazel are all at a science excursion. They split our class into two groups because it was too big to take everyone together. It's so unfair that Mrs Franks just went around the room, telling people they were group A or B. I was sitting between Edi and Hazel, so they were both put in group A and I ended up in group B. Jess was put in group A too, so they all went off together today, and I have to wait until next week.

I mean, it's not like I'm gagging to go to the Werribee

sewage plant, but even the stupidest excursions can be fun. And it's super annoying to be left out.

I'm not sure what to do at recess. I start walking down the breezeway, *trying* to look like I have a purpose. Then I see Mr Cartwright coming towards me.

'May I have a moment of your time, Olympia?' he asks.

I shrug and mutter a yes. This is really odd. He walks to the side of the breezeway so we won't get bowled over by the crowd coming towards us.

'I've taken the liberty of making an appointment for you with Ms Alisi in fourth period,' he says.

Everyone knows who Ms Alisi is, though we know her as Kelly, because she's given heaps of talks about bullying and stuff at assembly. She's the school counsellor.

'I believe a visit to her would be helpful, Olympia. You'll miss out on my maths class, but rest assured today's class will only be revision because so many students are away on the science excursion. Do you know where to find her?'

I nod. Kelly's office is in B Block, near the main entrance to the school. She says at assembly that her door is *always open.*

I feel a bit guilty. Last night, everything was really good at home. We just sat around watching TV like a normal family. And now I'm supposed to tell Kelly all about Mum and Dad's fights. I'm probably wasting her time.

V

When the bell rings for the fourth period, I'm not sure I want to go. It might be really awkward, trying to explain the stuff that goes on at home. But my friends are away from school and it's a chance to get out of maths, so I decide I'll give it a go.

I make my way to Kelly's office. There's a sign on the door that says:

In session. Please wait to be called.

But she has a sort of waiting room, where there's a seat and a coffee table with loads of cool magazines. I sit down and start flicking through the mags, catching up on celebrity goss. Then the door opens. I keep my head down, but I can still see who comes out. It's a girl from year eleven called Amy.

There are heaps of rumours about Amy that go through the school. I've heard that she cuts herself. I think the rumours are true too, because Amy walks around with the sleeves of her school jumper pushed up and you can actually see the scars. Cutting seems like a pretty weird thing to do in the first place, but I think it's even weirder that she doesn't care if everyone knows about it.

In a way, I get it. I guess Amy's pain is carved on her arms and wrists for everyone to see. Mine is just hidden away inside my body.

'Hey, Olympia,' says Kelly. 'Please come in.'

Kelly's office isn't like a regular office. There's no desk or the hard chairs we have in the classrooms. There are just two big, comfy lounge chairs and a beanbag. The chairs are side by side, but angled. As soon as I sit down on one of the lounge chairs, I get why. I can see Kelly's face, but I don't have to look at her directly. I think Kelly must have deliberately placed the chairs like that to give people the chance to talk while also having a bit of space. There's a box of tissues on a table next to my armchair. It makes me wonder how many kids might have cried in this room.

'Thanks for coming today,' Kelly says. 'I'd just like to start by letting you know that whatever you say in these sessions is private and confidential. The only exception to that would be if I believed you were being harmed by someone, or harming yourself. In that case, I would need to talk to someone.'

As soon as she says that, I feel antsy. No-one is actually harming me, and I'm not actually harming myself. Not like Amy, anyway. It makes me feel like I shouldn't really be here.

'Your teacher suggested you come here today because you've had some trouble finishing your homework and you said you were having some problems at home,' Kelly says. Her voice is gentle. 'Did you tell your teacher that?'

I shrug. 'Yeah, I guess so,' I begin. 'But it's not ... I mean, I don't really think it's that big a deal.'

Kelly tilts her head to the side. 'Olympia, my job is to talk to young people. There are no wrong things to talk about here. Everyone's situation is different and your experience is individual. If something matters *to you*, then it's worth talking about, okay?'

That makes me feel better. I'm more relaxed. Without thinking, I tuck my legs up on the chair under me. Kelly doesn't seem to mind.

'So, can you tell me a little bit about what home is like for you at the moment?'

I clear my throat. 'Well,' I begin, 'I'm pretty close with my mum.'

'Good,' Kelly says.

'But …' I say. I take a breath. 'But sometimes, my parents fight.'

Kelly nods. 'That must be difficult for you, Olympia. Do they argue in front of you?'

Now it's my turn to nod. I bite my lip.

'Yeah, they do. And after they fight, Dad sometimes goes to Aunty Kate's and stays there. Usually it's just for a few days. But every time he goes, it makes me wonder if it will be for good. It feels like he might never come back.'

'Ah, so when your parents argue, you feel like there's a chance that they'll break up,' Kelly says. 'That must be worrying.'

'It *is*,' I say. 'And the thing is, they don't even seem

to care that I worry about it. They don't try to hide their arguments; they just go at each other like I'm not even there.'

'How does that make you feel?' Kelly says. I don't think anyone has ever asked me that before.

'It makes me feel angry,' I say. 'And frustrated. And sad. And guilty.' Every time I think of a word that describes how I feel, another one comes along. I wonder if Kelly will think there are too many, or that they don't make sense all together, but when I look at her she's nodding. 'And confused,' I continue. 'Especially when Mum comes and talks to me about all Dad's faults afterwards. It shouldn't be my job to listen to that stuff.'

'So,' Kelly says slowly, like there's all the time in the world to talk like this. To talk about my life. 'Sometimes, I find it helpful to come up with a theory. Maybe you can tell me if I'm getting it right, or not really?' She pauses and draws her own legs under her. 'It sounds to me that when your parents argue in front of you, you feel they aren't considering how it makes you feel. Is that right?'

'Yes, that's right,' I say, and it feels good that she gets it.

She's put the feeling into words in a way that I haven't been able to. It's like she can *see* me in a way my parents don't. That everything I say and anything I might be thinking is important. It's a feeling I'm not used to. I have Kelly's undivided attention, and even if she's paid to do this, it still feels good.

'I also wonder,' she continues, 'whether you might feel that your mum comes to you for support when it's really her role as a mum to be the support for you. Is that right, Olympia?'

'Well, kind of. Except I love that Mum talks to me about most things like we're friends. But I just don't like the way she talks to me about Dad sometimes.'

'So, you love your relationship with your mum the way it is, except when it comes to talking about your dad's faults, right?'

I nod. I'm glad I can add that to her theory. I'd feel bad if I couldn't let her know that there are really good things about my family too. Kelly nods like she's really taking in that point. It also feels like I'm allowed to experiment with my words. That if I want to *unsay* anything that doesn't feel quite right, I can. Which makes talking about this stuff all seem really safe somehow.

'It's like …' I pause, searching for the right words. 'In a way, when Mum and Dad are fighting, it feels the same as it does when Mum dumps on me about Dad. Like they're not even thinking about me. Like I'm kind of invisible,' I finish.

'Mmmm,' Kelly says. 'So you feel like they're both not properly *aware* of you when they're arguing, and your mum also doesn't seem to be aware of how it upsets you when she talks to you about your dad. Is that right, Olympia?'

'Yes. That's it,' I say.

Kelly untucks her legs and puts her feet back on the floor. That's how I know the session is over.

'I'd like to see you again, Olympia,' she says. She writes an appointment time on a piece of paper and hands it to me. 'In the meantime, I'd like you to think about this. If you could say something to your parents and make them hear it, what would that be?' She pauses. 'When you've thought of what it is you want to say, write it down. And then, when you feel ready, I could help you communicate it, or you might even feel comfortable doing it on your own.'

I take the piece of paper. It's comforting to know I'll get to talk to Kelly again. I feel lighter somehow. As though it might be possible to sort out some of the tangled feelings that live inside me. And the day is just going to get better.

I've only got two more classes and then I get to join my friends at Edi's caravan.

Five

I'm excited about the caravan meeting. Edi's caravan is amazing. It's in her backyard and you can look through one of the little windows at the side and see her swimming pool. Her pool is way smaller than the one Veronica has on *Acacia Lane*, but at least Edi has one. She's so lucky to have her own private caravan space too, and I love that we get to share it when we have our meetings. And today, I'm feeling more pumped than usual because this 'emergency' meeting is going to be about *my* stuff for a change.

I walk down the driveway and pause. The caravan door

is open, and there's laughter coming from inside. Three types of laughter. Which means everyone has got here before me, even though I'm early.

Hazel appears in the doorway. As though it's *her* caravan.

'Hey, Limps,' she says, 'I've gotta go in the house to pee. Jess is cracking us up.'

I bite my lip. The laughter is still coming in waves. This isn't really what I expected, since this meeting is supposed to be serious.

But soon, Edi pokes her head through the curtains at the side of the caravan. She waves, and the next thing I know she's come out to meet me. She links her arm with mine and takes me behind the van.

'I just want you to know,' she says carefully, 'we got back to school from the excursion early and we were allowed to go home if we had a parent's consent. So, instead of everyone going back to their own houses and then over here, we all just came straight back to mine. That's why we're all here before you, okay?'

I feel myself relax a bit. It's nice that Edi made the effort to explain that to me. She wouldn't normally do that, and

I can tell she's trying to make sure I don't feel excluded. I give her a small smile so she knows that *I* know that she's trying.

'Okay,' I say, and we walk inside together.

Edi pulls me over to sit in our proper positions. I'm beside her on the lime-green bench seat. Jess slips in the other side of the table. Hazel comes back inside and slides in next to Jess.

'So, how was the excursion?' I ask, making sure my voice sounds casual.

'Well, of course it was lovely,' Edi says with a grin. 'The Werribee sewage plant. A dream excursion, really. So, so romantic. No wonder Jess found *luuurve* there.'

'Oh crap,' Jess says, putting her head in her hands. She looks completely clueless that she's even made a joke, but it sends Edi and Hazel off again.

'You should have been there, Limps,' Hazel says, which is really annoying because *clearly* I wasn't. But I plant a smile on my face. 'Tell her what happened, Jess.'

Jess nods and her ringlets spring up and down. 'Well, the guy was going on about the how poo is treated after it goes down our toilets and how it gets broken down on the way and …'

'Jess,' Hazel yells, holding up her hand as a stop sign. It's the signal we use when Jess goes off track. It happens a lot. 'Not about that! Tell her about Cheese Feet!'

'Let's not call him that anymore,' Jess says indignantly. 'His name is Chester, okay?'

I tap my foot under the table. I have a feeling Jess's story is going to take a while. Jess's stories tend to do that, and if there's a boy involved in this one, it could take even longer. I *am* interested, but I'm kind of deflated too. This meeting was supposed to be about me.

'Anyway,' Jess resumes, 'Adam comes up to me while the guy is talking about all the poo stuff, and he tells me that Chester likes me. He wants to know if I like him too. So I tell him that I can't really like Chester, because I don't even really know him. But Adam says that's the whole point, and that Chester is *interested* in getting to know me. Then, the sewage man stops talking and asks if there's anything we'd like to share with the whole group, and I shake my head. It's really embarrassing. When he finally starts talking again, I turn around and Chester is just standing there, staring at me.'

'He looked kind of grey,' Edi says.

Jess blows out a breath. 'He was sweaty too,' she says. 'He looked so nervous. Then he just blurted out, "Will you go out with me, Jess?" and his voice was all wobbly and I felt *so* sorry for him.' Now Jess screws up her face. 'I kind of *had* to say yes,' she says softly.

'So, now, Jess is going out with Cheese ...' Edi stops herself. 'Chester,' she corrects.

Even though I wouldn't go out with Chester Fealy if he was the last boy on earth, it's sort of disturbing that everyone else in my group has a boyfriend now. Someone who likes them. God, Jess was only number ten on the hot list. She was two below me!

'Ah, imagine being able to tell your children, and your grandchildren, where the romance started,' Hazel teases. She makes her face go all puckered up somehow, like an old woman. 'Darlings,' she says to her pretend children and grandchildren, 'we were high school sweethearts. It all began at the poo plant ...'

Even I can't help laughing along with Edi, but Jess grimaces.

'Eek,' she says. 'I just didn't want to hurt his feelings. I'm not really sure …' She starts going on about how she's probably made a big mistake agreeing to go out with Chester, and I'm beginning to think I'll never get a turn to talk.

I drift off as she's still talking. If it's *ever* going to be my turn, I need to say something about my parents that's more interesting than what actually happened the other night. I mean, it's nice that *Kelly* thinks whatever affects me is important, but she's not thirteen years old with a whole lot of stuff that happens all the time. Getting attention from friends is kind of like a competition. My real story isn't exciting enough. It's not full-on *or* terrible. And I can't even get a guy to like me or find me interesting. It's as though no matter which way I look at it, I'm not enough.

Last night, it was fun to think about telling the girls something full-on dramatic, but I never thought I'd do it for real. Now, though, I can feel something bubbling up inside me.

'All right, let's move on,' Edi says finally. 'We have an agenda.' She goes and gets four cans of Coke out of the caravan fridge and puts one down in front of us. We only get one can each per meeting, and Edi always makes sure we get it at the important part. It's good to know she's saved it for my time. That my thing is the main agenda for this meeting, and not the Jess and Chester stuff.

'Limps,' says Edi gently. 'Tell us what's been going on with you. At home.'

I take a sip of Coke. I need to make the most of this. My heart is pounding in my chest. And then, it just spills out of me.

'My dad is having an affair.'

'Oh my god.' Edi covers her mouth.

Jess slams down her can. 'That is just … the *worst*.'

All the girls are leaning towards me. Their eyes are wide. I have every *speck* of their attention. One hundred per cent. Now that my heart has stopped drumming, it's swollen up with their attention. I imagine this is what it might feel like to be Edi.

'So, where were you again, exactly?' Hazel asks. It's kind of like her to get bogged down in the details. I wonder, for a second, whether she might be testing me to see whether I'm telling the truth. But she won't catch me out. I might've been lying when I told them the *story* of what happened two nights ago, but I remember everything I've said. Now that it's done, I feel calm.

'In the supermarket car park,' I say. I'm not stupid enough to say I was carrying five million bags from a fashion store. For starters, I'm not spoilt like Veronica. Plus, nobody we know even drives a sports car. Mum's best friend Sandra drives a white Honda Accord, so that's what I used.

'And could you see properly from where you were? Are you *sure* they were actually hooking up?' Hazel says. 'Like, maybe they had a perfectly good reason to be together. Are you sure it wasn't just a normal goodbye kiss?'

'I *know* what hooking up is, Hazel,' I say.

Edi wraps her arms around me. 'God, Limps,' she says. That is so *full-on*. And *terrible*. Wasn't Sandra the one who came and stayed at your place for a while when your dad moved out?'

I nod. I think it's best not to say too much more now. There's a flash of something like guilt when Edi reminds me of how nice Sandra was when Dad went to Aunty Kate's. It threatens to ruin the good feeling I have.

'That's weird,' Hazel says. 'If Sandra and your dad were … well … seeing each other, why would she stay with you and your mum when he moved out? She'd be with your dad, wouldn't she?'

'Maybe it started after that,' Jess says. I'm relieved when Hazel seems to accept that. Honestly, she's like a *detective* sometimes.

'Are you going to tell your mum?' Hazel asks. 'We could all go with you.'

I shake my head, maybe a little too quickly, but the idea really cuts into my happy, full feeling. 'No. Mum can't know. It would *kill* her,' I say.

'Yeah, she'd be crushed, but isn't it better that she knows the truth?' Hazel continues. 'Like, it's her *husband* and her *best friend.* A best friend is someone you should be able to trust! I think she'd want to know.'

'If I told her, my parents would definitely break up,' I say and I hope that's enough to stop Hazel on this path, but she keeps going.

'Sometimes, breaking up is the right thing to do,' she says. 'Like, when my parents broke up, it was really horrible for me and my sister for a while, but we got used to it.'

I really wish Hazel would shut up. It's like she thinks she knows everything.

'Hazel, you were, like, *six,* when your parents broke up,' I say. 'You probably didn't even *understand* what was going on.'

Hazel leans back in her seat, as though what I've said makes her want to back away from me. At least it makes her stop talking.

'I think,' Edi says, grabbing my hand, and frowning at Hazel, 'that we should all do whatever Limps wants us to do. She needs to be our first priority. We have to be there for her, whatever happens. Right, girls?' she says.

Jess agrees immediately. Then Hazel looks at me. I can see that she realises she has to be nice to me. After all, I'm going through *hell.* Eventually, she nods too.

'Right,' Hazel says.

Edi stares at me like I'm the only other person in the caravan, and gives my hand a squeeze. She's *totally* taking my side. And with Edi on my side, I feel really powerful.

For once, everyone is paying attention to me.

It feels amazing.

Six

I'm really glad I chose art as my elective this term. I love it, of course, but it's not just that. The girls have been so good to me the last couple of days, and it still feels great. But this *thing* I've created about Dad and Sandra is starting to feel complicated. Whenever the girls bring it up, I get a nervous jittery feeling, and they bring it up much more than I thought they would. So, it's nice to have art class without them, just for a break.

I sit down at my table and take my drawing from the hardcover folder that protects it. Myra stands behind me, looking at the drawing I've done of me, Edi, Jess and Hazel in the caravan. Myra is by far my favourite teacher. She lets us call her by her first name, and she's really chilled. I bet she never goes running. She even lets us have music playing while we work. At the moment, we're doing portraits. I'm the only one in our class who's attempting more than one portrait at a time.

'Wow, Olympia. That's coming along so *beautifully*,' she says. She lifts my drawing and gets everyone's attention. 'Look at how Olympia has done the shading,' she says. 'See how she's created depth and dimension with her strokes?'

As she puts my drawing back in front of me, I smile at her. It's nice to be used as a *good* example. It adds to the feeling that life is swinging my way, for once.

I glance to the side. Not to be mean or anything, but Anya's self-portrait is pretty amateur. For starters, she's done her nose as two nostrils, flat on the page. Her eyes have no pupils and her hair is super thin. The Anya beside me is way prettier than the monster on the page, that's for sure.

The next thing I know, Nick is behind us, a hand on

each of our chairs. It's freaky how he does stuff like that. Nick doesn't have any idea of personal space, but after what he said to Mr C when I was upset in maths, I don't really mind.

'Your picture is the best, Olympia,' he says, pointing at my drawing. Then he points at Anya's. 'Yours isn't good.'

'Hey, Nick, go easy,' Anya says, but she's laughing. The thing is, Nick just says what he thinks. I know he hasn't intended to give me a compliment, or to criticise Anya. He just tells it as he sees it.

'I read a book once,' Nick continues, oblivious to Anya's protest, 'where this guy was such a good drawer that whatever he drew came to life. That's what your picture is like, Olympia. You should draw you and your friends with wings or something, and then you might all be able to fly.'

'Thanks, Nick,' I say, pulling my chair forward a bit so his hand isn't stuck behind me. 'That's a good idea.'

'Can you draw me too?' he asks.

'Yeah, sure,' I tell him. 'After I finish this.'

'Can you draw me, but make me really muscly?' says Nick. 'Oh, yeah!' he exclaims. 'Make me really muscly like the Incredible Hulk. That would be way cool. Imagine coming to life like that! I'd be the strongest guy in the whole school!'

'The Incredible Hulk is green,' I remind him.

'Cool,' Nick says.

I give him a smile. 'Let's see how we go.'

But Nick has already returned to his seat.

'Jesus, Olympia. Dog. Lead. Treats. It's pretty basic,' Dad says as we pull into the car park where obedience class is being held. 'I don't have time to go back home. I've got an important meeting, and if it doesn't go well, we'll lose the contract. You'll have to see if you can borrow a lead.' He leans over me and opens the passenger door.

I don't look back after I get out with Cricket under my arm. Dad is so mean sometimes, when he's stressed about work. I forget *one thing* and all the stuff he's said about me being mature enough to take Cricket to obedience school goes out the window. It makes me feel better about what

I've said about him and Sandra, actually.

I'm still fuming when a boy in a Kilmore High blazer walks towards me. He looks kind of familiar, but I'm not sure why. Cricket struggles to get out of my arms, and starts barking at the basset hound with big droopy ears on the end of the guy's lead.

'Hey, your dog isn't going to learn much if you don't let him out of your arms,' he says.

'Her,' I say huffily. 'Cricket is a girl. And I've … well … I've forgotten her lead.'

'Don't worry about it,' he says. 'Hang on.' As he leans over to unclip his dog's lead, his hair flops down over his face. And then I realise why he's familiar. It's Cute Art-Store Boy!

His dog lead is half leather and half chain. Somehow, he splits it in two and hands me the chain part. I put Cricket down and try to find the loop in her collar to attach the lead. It's not easy, since she keeps wriggling. Finally I manage to get her on.

'Thanks,' I say, looking at the boy properly for the first time. He's gorgeous.

'Yeah, no problem. I'm Alec, and this is Barney.' He points at the basset hound. 'Barney's a *he,*' he adds cheekily.

'I'm Olympia,' I say. 'And, as you know, Cricket is a *she.*'

'I think our dogs like each other,' he says. When I look down, I see Barney and Cricket going around in circles, sniffing each other's bums.

I feel a wave of heat passing through my face, and hope he can't see it. 'We'd better hurry up, or they'll get in trouble for being late.'

V

I didn't expect dog obedience school to be fun. But it is. Alec and I stay next to each other as we teach the dogs to heel. We let them off the leads for this. The idea is that you carry around treats, holding them out just behind you so the dogs will follow. When they do the right thing, they get their treat.

'Hey, Olympia,' Alec says as we walk, 'wouldn't it be cool if our teachers taught us like this?'

I smile. 'Yeah, but not if they used liver treats.'

Alec grins. 'I reckon it should be more like, "Nice work on the comprehension questions, Alec. Here's a Mars bar!"'

I join in the game. 'Or, "Excellent work on your maths exercise, Olympia. Here's a Coke!"' The thought of Mr C offering Cokes around the classroom makes me laugh out loud.

'Oh, don't they do that at your school?' Alec laughs with me.

'Nope, that must just be for the smart people at Kilmore High,' I tease. As I say it, I notice that Barney has stayed behind. He's more interested in something on the ground than Alec's treats.

'Yep. That must just be for us smart people,' Alec grins. Then he leans into me. 'Poor old Barney is repeating,' he says. 'He failed obedience school last time, but I don't hold that against him. He has other qualities. For example, he's a very good *listener*.'

I love that he says that. I imagine Alec confiding in Barney the same way I confide in Cricket.

'By the way,' Alec says. 'Not everyone at Kilmore is super smart. Some of us get in just because we live in the right zone.' He whispers it like it's a secret. Just for me.

V

'I can't believe how much energy Cricket has,' Alec says after the lesson.

'I can't believe how *little* energy Barney has,' I say. Both of us laugh as we look at the dogs. Barney is curled up on the grass like he's knackered from the lesson and Cricket is diving at him from all angles, trying to get him up to play.

I glance towards the car park. Mum isn't here yet.

'I'd better give you your lead back,' I say.

Alec tilts his head to the side. 'You can borrow it if you like,' he says. 'You can give it back next week. Or maybe we could meet at the skate park, since it's sort of in between our houses?'

'Sure,' I say. I only mentioned where I live once during the lesson. Alec has remembered. It's a nice feeling. But then I realise I've said 'sure' before he's even mentioned when he wants to meet. As though I'm available *all the time.* I'm glad, at least, that I haven't mentioned seeing him at the art supplies store. That would make me seem kind of freaky, I think.

'I usually take Barney on Saturday mornings around eleven. Would that be cool with you?'

Alec smiles his cute smile and I feel fine again. Better than fine, actually. Walking dogs isn't exactly a date or anything, but I don't think Alec would have asked me if he didn't want my company.

Oh my god. *Maybe a boy finally likes me*, I think. *And I didn't even have to try.*

'I'll see you there,' I say.

Seven

It's Friday night. Since we had our caravan meeting earlier in the week, we've decided to watch a DVD at Hazel's place.

Her house pongs of scented candles, but I'm glad to get out of my own house. Last night, Dad was in one of those moods he gets in, crashing around the place like everything he looked at, including me and Mum, was annoying. He didn't need to say his meeting had gone badly. It was just there, in the air.

I ended up going into my room. I did three drafts of

the thing Kelly asked me to do to help *communicate* with my parents. None of them was quite right and I didn't go and give it to them or anything, but it did make me feel a bit better. Because one day I *might* get it right, and maybe then I'll be able to tell them how I'm feeling.

After that, I lay in bed and started my drawing of Nick. So far, I've just done bits and pieces. I haven't decided whether I'll draw him as he actually is, or as the Incredible Hulk. I think portraits are supposed to reveal something real about you, not show what you're not.

Anyway, I'm glad it's the weekend now, and I'm sitting here with my friends.

'So, did you get *Mean Girls*?' I ask Hazel. I settle on the couch next to Edi, and Hazel doesn't even say anything about it. She flops into the beanbag closest to the TV and Jess sits in another.

'Yep,' Hazel replies. As she slides in the DVD, her mum's boyfriend appears in the doorway to the lounge room. He's really weird-looking, with long dreadlocks that hang down his back, and he's always barefoot. But there's something peaceful about him. I can't imagine him moodily crashing around like my dad, anyway.

'Hey, you guys feel like some corn fritters and relish?' he asks.

'Oooh yeah, thanks, Jason,' Edi answers. 'They're the best.'

'That's because they're made with *love* and *tenderness*, hey, Jason?' Hazel says. She's got an innocent expression on her face, as though she's being completely sincere, but we can't help giggling.

Jason tilts his head to the side, like he can't figure out if Hazel is making fun of him. He walks back into the kitchen.

I get a prickly feeling inside me, wondering when Edi has tried Jason's corn fritters before, because *I* haven't. Which means Edi and Hazel have hung around together without me some other time. I'm pretty sure it would have been before I told them Dad was having an affair, though. I think they've always tried to include me since then.

'Let's wait for the fritters before we start the movie,' Edi says. 'Tell us more about the guy from obedience school, Limps.' I get a feeling that she's trying to distract me and I wonder if maybe she hangs out here eating Jason's corn fritters without me all the time, but I decide to let it go.

'Well, his name is Alec and he goes to Kilmore High,' I say.

'Which must mean he's brainy,' Jess interrupts. 'I knew a kid once who sat the entrance exam for Kilmore, and he said it was severe. His name was Justin Smart. Which is pretty funny, because he wasn't actually *smart* enough to ace the exam and he ended up having to go to …'

'Jess,' Hazel laughs. She holds up one hand. With the other, she's pressing buttons on the DVD player, like something's not working properly.

I don't feel like saying anything about Alec getting into Kilmore because he lives in the area. So instead I say, 'We just got along really well.' I bite my lip before adding, 'I'm actually catching up with him tomorrow morning at the skate park.'

'That's awesome, Limps,' Edi says. 'Just what you need to get your mind off … all that other stuff.'

'Yeah,' Jess agrees. 'It's good, Limps. No offence, but it

is kind of weird that absolutely no-one has liked you at our school. Like, *nobody*.'

'Jess!' Hazel says.

'What?' Jess says.

I shake my head, but I'm smiling. That last comment is so Jess. She really doesn't get why Hazel is protesting. But it doesn't matter. Finally, things are starting to work out for me. Finally, I'm getting attention from my friends *and* from a boy.

'I'm just telling the truth,' Jess says with a pout.

'Yeah, well, maybe you could consider telling a bit *less* of it,' Edi advises her. Then she turns to me. 'Maybe we could all come and meet you at the skate park tomorrow? With Archie and Leo.'

Actually, I think I'd rather meet with Alec by myself. I wouldn't mind having some time to get to know him by myself. But before I have to answer, Jason comes in with corn fritters.

Hazel takes a bite of hers, and clicks at the DVD player again. 'Girls, we have a *situation*,' she says seriously. 'The stupid DVD player isn't working.'

We all groan. We've seen this movie heaps of times before, but we never get sick of it.

'Yeah, it hasn't been working all week,' Jason says over our groans. 'I tried to do my yoga DVD the other day and –'

'Jason!' Hazel says. 'Why didn't you say anything?'

Jason shrugs. 'Oh, I thought it might, you know, heal itself.'

The look Hazel gives us behind Jason's back is pretty funny. A combination of crossed eyes and a sticking-out tongue. Jason leaves the lounge room and Hazel's big sister Romy appears at the doorway. If I could have a big sister, I'd get one like Romy. She's great and she looks really pretty, even in her pyjamas and ugg boots.

'Hey, Roms,' Hazel says, 'do you have anything good recorded on Foxtel? The DVD is stuffed.'

Romy leans on the doorframe. 'Mmm,' she says. 'I've got the latest episode of *Acacia Lane*. Check if …'

I don't hear the rest of what Romy's saying. I'm vaguely aware of the others discussing whether to watch it or do something else altogether. But their words just float around me like mist. I become aware of my heartbeat. The beat becomes a dull thump, completely taking over my insides.

'Limps, Limps, earth to Limps,' Edi says, waving her hand in front of my face.

'You haven't seen it, have you? None of us have.'

I shake my head. There's no way I could talk right now. I put my hand to my chest, to stop my heart from leaping out.

'Okay, *Acacia Lane* it is,' Hazel says.

V

I'm hardly even here. My body is sitting on the couch, next to Edi. But there's nothing much inside me. Just corn fritters and fog and fear.

I look at the screen, but I don't see what's happening. My skin is clammy, as though every little pore is seeping beads of sweat.

I'm dimly aware of the girls commenting on Veronica's clothes. They're all really tuned in. Thoughts float through the empty space inside me like astronauts.

These girls are my only friends, really. I know other girls at school, of course. But not the way I know Edi, Jess and Hazel. Together, we're the popular group. There was a time when that mattered to me more than our actual friendships. But it's not the main thing now. We've confided in each other. We've discussed periods and boys and other people at school. I've told them stuff I would never tell anyone else. And they've been so kind to me lately. But now, I can only think one thing.

They are going to hate me.

That thought pushes me over the edge of the cliff I've been teetering on ever since I told the lie. But the fall seems to go forever. In the end, though, I know I'll hit the ground. In ten minutes from now, I'll be splattered.

I really will be invisible, after this. It won't just be that I'm not quite good enough. I'll be one of the tragics who wanders around at lunchtime, alone. Maybe I'll just hang out with Kelly all the time, tucked away in her office.

There she is. Veronica, finding the credit card wrapped in a bow on her kitchen bench. Not long now. I tuck my legs underneath me on the couch.

There she is. Coming out of Juicy Couture with her fifty million shopping bags. Everyone's eyes are glued to the screen.

Now the music amps up. My heart matches the tempo. *Thump. Thump. Thump.*

There she is. Watching as her dad and her mum's best friend hook up.

It's over. The show. My friendships.

I put my head in my hands, peering through my open fingers. The *thump, thump, thump* is pulsing in my temples. I imagine going back in time, somehow unsaying what I've told them. But it's impossible. I'm stuck right here, with time creeping forward.

No-one talks. Hazel gets up out of her beanbag, walks over to the TV and switches it off. She turns around. She walks over to me. It's odd that she kneels on the carpet in front of me. 'Olympia,' she says.

I take my hands off my eyes and lower them into my lap. Wait for my life to end.

'I'm so sorry. That must have been awful for you. If we'd known … if any of us knew what was going to be in that program, we would never have put it on. We *never* would have done that to you.'

The girls are all around me now. Gathered together in a huddle with me at the centre.

My sobs are real.

Eight

It's hard to get to sleep that night. The *Acacia Lane* thing could have turned out so differently. I don't even want to think about it. I feel like I'm still falling down, down, down that cliff face, and I haven't hit the bottom yet. But there's also a nagging sense that the splat might happen at any time. When I least expect it.

In the morning, I get a text from Edi.

Hi Limps, going to watch Archie this morning cos there's try-outs for some soccer league. H and Leo coming too. It's a big deal for A, or I'd definitely be at skate park. Ok???

I look at the screen, and even though my stomach scrunches knowing Edi and Hazel are hanging out together, I feel a bit relieved that I'll get to see Alec by myself. Last night was pretty intense, and I definitely don't want to talk about anything to do with Dad and Sandra or *Acacia Lane* today. Plus, those three question marks make me feel like Edi is kind of asking my permission, which is *something*.

KK, I text back and start getting ready.

V

Alec is already at the skate park when I get there. I see him standing by the graffiti wall. Barney has found a patch of sun, and he's making little circles to flatten the grass around him so he can lie down. He follows reluctantly as Alec starts walking towards me.

Cricket goes nuts when she sees Barney. It's a bit embarrassing that she's acting so keen, but at least it gives us something to talk about straight away.

'Hey, Olympia,' Alec says. 'I think we'd better let them off their leads.'

I look down and see that our two leads are all tangled as Barney starts warming up to Cricket's play-fighting game.

Alec's hand brushes my arm as he unclips Barney. It feels good. As soon as we set them free, the dogs start racing in circles and rolling around in the grass.

'They're pretty cute together,' Alec says.

I look at him properly for the first time today. He's wearing grey skinny jeans, a blue V-neck T-shirt and maroon Vans. The dogs aren't the only things that are cute around here.

'Come with me?' says Alec. 'I want to show you something.'

The dogs follow us as we walk together. I don't care where we're going. I don't even think about what Alec might want to show me. I'm just happy to be here at the skate park with Alec. Who happens to go to Kilmore High. And who happens to be incredibly hot.

When we get to the graffiti wall, Alec points at something. It's an amazing stencil graffiti of a lazy-looking basset hound with extra-long ears and droopy eyes. Underneath are the words, *Stop hounding me.*

'Oh my god, Alec,' I breathe. 'It's awesome. That's Barney, isn't it?'

Alec smiles. I count the freckles across his nose. Twelve. It seems like the perfect number of freckles.

'Did you do that?' I ask.

Alec nods. 'Yeah. Do you like it?'

'Of course!' I say. Alec smiles at me and I'm feeling sort of embarrassed, so I point to another piece of graffiti on the wall that I know was painted by Hazel's boyfriend, Leo. 'I know the guy who did that one.' It's a picture of a girl in a bikini with a sash that says, *Miss Everything*. It's a strange picture in a way. Everything about the girl is in proportion except for her giant feet. At the bottom, Leo has written, *Filling the big shoes.*

'Do you know Leo?' I ask Alec. 'He did this for my friend Hazel.' I watch as Alec studies it.

'It's cool,' says Alec. 'I've never met him, but I recognise his stuff. It's pretty random sometimes, but he's really good. Maybe you can introduce us sometime?'

'Sure,' I say, and I try to sound casual, but I love the way Alec just takes it for granted that we'll see each other again.

In my mind, I picture introducing him to my friends. This cute, artistic boy. I feel kind of puffed up just thinking about it.

I look more closely at Leo's graffiti. Alec is right – it *is* good. 'There's no way I could do something like that with graffiti paints. I like painting, but usually I just draw.'

'Oh, yeah?' Alec cocks an eyebrow. 'You draw?'

'Yeah, a bit,' I say. I get out my phone and show him a photo I've taken on the progress of my drawing of Nick.

As he looks at the photo, I can tell that he thinks it's good. Even though I haven't filled in the facial features yet, I think I've captured the way Nick stands when he's excited, with his hands outstretched in front of him like he wants to grab whatever experiences he can.

'Geez, Olympia,' he says finally, and he's really looking at me now. He shakes his head. 'You draw a *bit*? I have a feeling you might draw *a lot*. Either that, or you just got lucky with your genes. Like, *talented*.' He tilts his head and his hair flops over his eye. I want to reach out and tuck it away. 'That's going to be … That's amazing.'

'Thanks,' I say.

Alec clicks his fingers. '*That's* where I've seen you before,' he says. 'I've been trying to figure out where I know you from. You go to the art supplies store, right? Digby's?'

'Yep,' I say. It feels good to know that he's noticed me too. 'I think I might have seen you there a couple of times too,' I admit.

'Don't you love it?' he says. 'There's something about that store that's so relaxing. Like it's its own little world.'

'Exactly,' I say, and it's amazing to think Alec feels the same way I do.

Just then, Cricket jumps up in front of me, trying to get my attention. It's funny when Barney tries jumping too. He hardly gets off the ground.

Alec laughs. He lifts Barney up and then drops him down, like he's helping him to jump. It's so cute, watching them. I guess I've never really had a connection like this with a boy. It just feels right.

When Barney starts looking tired, Alec turns to me. 'I guess we should get going, huh? But this has been ... well ... it's been nice. For me, that is.'

'For me too,' I say quickly and I don't even feel that

awkward for saying it, because Alec's eyes light up.

'I'm away next week, but maybe we should meet here to walk the dogs every Saturday?'

'Yes, we so should,' I say. And now I don't even feel worried about sounding too keen. Not one bit.

V

After Alec leaves, I walk around the skate park with Cricket to give her a bit more of a run than the one she got with Barney.

As I'm about to leave, I see Jess and her dog Frodo. She flashes past me and starts running backwards.

'Hey, Limps,' she yells. 'Late for basketball. See you Monday.'

I give her a wave. I'm not thinking about school. Not yet, anyway. I refuse to.

Because what's happened today fills me up to the brim.

Nine

I'm not exactly happy about missing out on art class first period on Monday morning. But in some ways it's okay, because Edi, Jess and Hazel won't even know about my counselling session. I'm actually pretty keen to go. My thoughts have been seesawing all weekend.

I tried to stay focused on the nice bit, the Alec bit. But as soon as I think about him, I want to tell my friends about him. And then I remember how scared I felt while I was watching *Acacia Lane*. And just when I think I might have found the right words to talk to Mum, I get a flash of panic that the girls will find me out. It's truly exhausting.

I hope Kelly can help.

'Hi, Olympia. How have you been since our last session?' Kelly asks straight away.

This time, I sit in the beanbag. '*Some* things have been good,' I say, thinking of Alec.

'I'm glad to hear that,' Kelly says. 'Did you start thinking about what you might like to say to your parents to get them to hear you?'

'I did,' I say. 'I haven't actually said anything to them yet, though.'

'Would you like me to look at what you came up with, Olympia?' Kelly asks.

I hand her a piece of paper with what I've written so far. My hand shakes as I give it to her.

'Olympia, is there something else you'd like to discuss?' She says it as though she knows already what's happened. Which, of course, she doesn't. The thing is, she's the only person in the world I can talk to about this. And even though I've tried to squash down the fear inside me, it just seems to take up more and more space. I'm even afraid of seeing the girls today. I've been afraid ever since I told the lie. It's horrible. I need to get it out of me.

I move the beanbag slightly so my back is to Kelly. I'm not sure why I do that, but it feels better if she's not looking at me. Then it all gushes out of me. The lie. Where I got it from. How my friends have tried to help me.

Kelly doesn't interrupt. She just lets me talk until I'm finished. Eventually, I turn the beanbag back towards her, but I keep looking down at the ground.

'You seem very angry,' Kelly says, and I realise how I must have sounded. 'It sounds like you have to work hard to maintain your position with your friends. Does that make you feel angry, Olympia?'

'Yes!' I say, grabbing on to that idea like it's a lifeboat. '*Nobody* pays attention to me. That's why I had to do it.' My eyes are pricking with tears, but I don't want to start crying. Kelly slides the box of tissues towards me.

'We have choices, though,' Kelly says gently. 'And you probably have some mixed feelings about the choice you made, Olympia. On the one hand, it feels good to get the attention you crave. On the other, you might feel ashamed and guilty about how you've got that attention. How do you feel about what you told your friends?'

I take a deep breath. 'I feel *sick*,' I say, and it comes out sounding really small. Now I know the reason I had my back to Kelly while I told her about it. I'm so ashamed about what I've done, and she knows it. All of a sudden, that box of tissues looks like an invitation to cry. And I'm doing it. I'm crying.

'I want to take it back,' I say between sobs. 'I want to *unsay* it, Kelly.'

For a moment, there's hope in the air between us. Like Kelly might have a magic potion that can unsay the things I've said. To fix this sick jumped-off-the-edge-of-a-cliff feeling I carry around inside me. Kelly is blurry through my tears.

'Unfortunately, there's no way to do that, Olympia.'

Hearing that makes me cry harder, because I know it's too true. Maybe you can unsay things inside a counselling session, but you can't do it in real life. What I've said is going to be said forever. I blow my nose and wait for Kelly to continue.

'I guess what we have to do now is to work out the consequences of keeping your story going,' Kelly says. 'What do you think might happen if you never correct it?'

'My friends might find out,' I say, and the fear of that happening seems to swallow up everything else inside me. 'If that happens, they'll think I'm a liar, and I won't even *have* friends anymore.'

'And what if you tell them the truth?' Kelly says. 'Sometimes things have to get worse before they can get better.'

I cross my arms and bite my lip in frustration. Kelly should know that telling the truth now isn't an option. If I admit what I've done, my friends will think I'm a complete nut job. They'll never trust me again. Things wouldn't just get worse, my friendships would be over.

'It's a difficult dilemma you're in, Olympia,' Kelly says. 'But perhaps you could figure out a way to explain why you made up the story in the first place? Perhaps your friends could forgive you if you found the right words.'

I dry my eyes. I've expected too much from Kelly. She's nice and everything, but she obviously doesn't get it.

But I think I have an idea that might make things better. I can do it tonight when the girls come to my place to finish our drama assignment. Then the sick feeling will go away, and I'll figure out a better way of getting their attention that isn't so scary.

'Thanks, Kelly,' I say. 'I'll think about it.'

Ten

As soon as the girls arrive at my house that afternoon, I herd them into my room.

I show them the cover I've drawn for our drama script. It's pretty good, but the girls are more interested in talking about what happened at the skate park yesterday. I tell them all about our conversation at the graffiti wall, about how much Alec and I seem to have in common. Hazel is excited to introduce him to Leo. And then I tell them how Alec suggested we meet up every Saturday.

'Oh my god, you're so lucky,' Jess says. 'Chester and

I have zero to talk about. It's so unfair. All you guys have someone you actually *like*.'

It feels good, for once, being on the same level as Edi and Archie and Hazel and Leo. Well, similar. It's not like anything has happened between me and Alec. It's not like we're actually going out together, but whatever it is, at least it's *something*.

'I guess you're going to have to dump Chester, Jess,' I say. Then, I take a deep breath. This is about the best opportunity I'm going to get to lead into telling the girls that Dad and Sandra are over. I'm going to say that I saw a text on Dad's phone, and that's how I know. I can't tell them the truth, but at least if they don't think Dad's having an affair, it kind of *undoes* the damage. Then, I'll be able to get rid of the sick feeling.

But just as I open my mouth to tell the story, there's a knock at our front door. Then, I hear a voice. It's the same bright, bubbly voice that I've known forever.

Sandra's voice.

'Okay, I guess you guys should get going now,' I say, hoping my voice isn't too wobbly. But the girls just ignore me. They're too involved in talking about how Jess should go about dumping Chester.

'You could just tell Chester you like him as a friend, and you don't want to ruin the friendship,' Hazel suggests.

I hear a laugh from the kitchen. I strain my ears to listen over the top of the girls talking. I hear Dad's voice, though I can't hear what he's saying. Then I hear Sandra say, 'Let's open a bottle of wine.'

Oh my god. They're settling in.

'He wouldn't believe that,' Jess sighs, 'cos we're not actually friends. Whichever way I do it, I'm going to hurt his feelings. It totally sucks.'

'Maybe you could tell him you're too busy with …'

I can't focus on what Edi is saying now. Because there are footsteps coming up the hallway. Then there's a knock on my bedroom door. It opens.

'Hey, girls,' Mum says. 'How is everyone? Edi, great boots. Are they the ones you were wearing when you got photographed for the paper?'

'Yep,' Edi says. 'I like your dress too.' Mum's dress is nice. It's white with blue stars and it comes down almost

97

to her knees. She's so much younger than the other mums, and it's cool that she can talk fashion with my friends. Well, normally it is. Right now, I'm praying that she'll just go and leave us alone so I can get the girls out of here.

'I've made some snacks,' Mum says, ruining that hope. 'Sandra's dropped in. Why don't you girls come and join us?'

'They have to go now, Mum,' I say.

'No, that's fine,' Edi says. 'We can stay for a bit longer. Can't we, Hazel and Jess?'

When I look back, all of the girls are staring at me. Three pairs of eyes are narrowed and harsh at the sound of Sandra's name. Like they're preparing for battle. They look at each other and then back to me. To show that they're ready to support me.

I try to smile, but it's more of a grimace.

V

'Sandy, this is Edi, and Jess and Hazel,' Mum says as we walk into the kitchen.

Sandra gives me two thumbs up as a hello and then

extends her hand towards Edi. It's really awkward when Edi crosses her arms. I can see Sandra is confused, but then, she probably just thinks teenagers don't shake hands anymore. She doesn't try with the others. Well, she wouldn't, really, since their arms are crossed just like Edi's.

'Sandy has been my absolute best buddy for …' Mum starts and then pauses to consider how long.

Hazel scoffs, but Mum doesn't seem to realise.

'Gosh … for how long, Sandy?' she continues, refilling both of their wine glasses. The two of them clink glasses.

'Since we were about your age,' Sandra says, looking around at all of us. My friend's faces are grim.

'Ah, so you …' Jess does a little cough, 'really *trust* each other?' she says, directing a glare at Sandra that makes me freeze. If *Jess* is acting like this, then god help Sandra if the others start.

Sandra tilts her head to the side, as though she thinks Jess's question is odd. But she answers anyway. Sandra is too nice not to answer. At the moment, I wish she wasn't.

'Yes, of course,' she says. 'There's nothing in the world like a close girlfriend. Boys may come and go but – '

'Hey, watch it, Sandra,' Dad says in a jokey voice as he comes into the kitchen.

'… and come back, of course, Jimmy,' Sandra says, filling a wine glass and handing it to Dad. I know it's just her being good-natured. When she looked after us while Dad was gone, she never said anything bad about him. She was just there for me and Mum.

But the girls must be thinking she's playing some sort of evil game, with my mum as the victim. No-one even takes a biscuit when Mum offers them around. It's as though they don't want anything to distract them from focusing on what seems to be going on. Of course, Mum, Dad and Sandra just chat away like nothing's wrong.

'Hey, Sandy,' Dad says after a while. 'I got *that part* for your car.' He gives Sandra a wink so we can see but Mum can't. I can practically feel my friends' bodies stiffen.

'Come out to the garage, and we'll see if it's right,' he says to Sandra. Then he turns to me, his eyes wide. 'Why don't you come too, Limps, since you'll be driving someday?'

It's completely lame, but I know what's going on. Every

year, Sandra gives Dad advice on what to get Mum for her birthday.

'Okay, have you got all your stuff?' I say to my friends, 'I'll walk you to the door.'

'Oh, I'll do that, Limps,' Mum says. 'I want to ask Edi where she got her boots.'

I breathe in. It *should* be okay. It's not like the girls would say anything to Mum without me there. And I know Sandra will wait for me if I don't go right away.

The mood in this kitchen is intense, even if the adults don't realise it. I've got to get Sandra out of here before something gives. So I walk out to the garage with Dad and Sandra.

Sandra's Honda Accord is parked next to our ute. Dad, Sandra and I stand next to the open window, where warm sunlight filters through into the garage.

'So,' Sandra says. 'I've got the best idea for Vanny's birthday.' She's trying to whisper, but her whisper is as bubbly as her regular voice. 'Last week, when we went shopping, she saw a pair of earrings and a necklace that she really liked. They weren't that expensive. I think she'd love it if you gave her the earrings, Jimmy,' she says. She turns to me. 'And you could follow up with the necklace, Limps. Perfecto.'

'Sounds good. Where were they?' Dad asks.

'You know the little store in the Westland Mall?' Sandra asks. 'Cargo?'

Dad shakes his head, but I know it. Edi bought a bracelet there. 'Yep, I know it,' I say. 'You'll just have to show us which one she liked.'

Then a shadow falls across the garage floor. I look and see three heads at the window. I make an excuse to leave, then go out into the backyard. The girls are there, crouching down. There's nothing I can do.

'I'll meet you there, Jimmy.' Sandra's voice bubbles through the window. 'How about Friday night?'

'Yeah, I reckon I can swing that,' Dad says. 'I could always tell Vanny that I'm working late.'

I look around. At three mouths, gaping open in horror.

'All right, Jimmy, it's a date,' Sandra says, and she might as well have said, *Let's go to a hotel room and have sex*, as far as the girls are concerned.

V

As Dad and Sandra go back inside, the girls flop backwards in a row on the grass. I keep crouching. Jess and Hazel hold me by the elbows and ease me down.

'Is she okay?' Edi asks, as though I'm not here.

'I think she might be in shock. Are you in shock, Limps?'

I shrug. Maybe I *am* in shock. Mainly that I've got myself into this situation. The girls definitely won't let this go now. I can feel it in my bones.

'Limps, I'm so sorry,' Hazel says.

'I just can't believe it,' Jess adds.

'That's because it's *unbelievable*,' says Edi.

They keep going on, but I don't even know who's saying what. It's all a mish-mash.

'I feel like climbing in the window and smashing her stupid Honda Accord to pieces.'

'Yeah, but it's not only Sandra. Like, she's obviously the *worst* best friend in history, and I can't believe she's making a date with Olympia's dad almost right under her mum's *nose*. But it's him too. How could he do that to your mum?'

'It's even more horrible than what happened on *Acacia Lane* and it's *real life!*'

'It's so, so, so wrong.'

As they talk, Sandra's car starts up. We can hear Mum shouting her goodbyes from the driveway. Then, Dad's ute starts up. He's probably just nicking up to the shops to get stuff for dinner, but I know the girls will assume he's driving off to hook up with Sandra somewhere.

It's my fault they think that.

My hands are in my lap, curled into fists. Jess puts her hand over my left one and then Hazel and Edi layer theirs on top.

'Limps,' Edi says, 'you have no choice now. It's gone too far. Your mum *has* to know.'

'You have to tell her, Limps. It's the right thing to do,' Jess declares. She stands up and the others stand up too.

They pull me to my feet. I've got pins and needles from crouching for so long. I can barely feel my legs. But, still, the girls are pulling me forward, back into the house.

And suddenly, I can't stand it anymore. The stupid secret. The sick feeling. The constant stomach-lurch of having jumped off a cliff, and knowing at any minute I'll be splattered onto the ground.

'Wait,' I say. 'There's something I need to tell you.'

Eleven

I take the girls over to the outdoor setting in our backyard. It's a rickety round table with some fold-out chairs.

Cricket comes out the doggy door and straight over to me. She sits at my feet. I'm glad to have her there.

The girls are waiting for me to say something. I'm about to land, finally. I'm about to be *splattered*. I don't have a choice. I can't avoid it anymore.

'It's not what you think,' I begin. 'Dad and Sandra are meeting up to get Mum's birthday present. You guys just heard the part where they were making a time to do it.'

The girls are quiet. I can tell they're not buying what I've said.

'And I just might have, sort of, *exaggerated* what happened with Dad and Sandra the other night,' I continue.

'Oh, Limps,' Edi says. I can tell she's still feeling sorry for me. That she's thinking I want to backtrack because the situation is too intense. Not because the situation *doesn't exist*. 'It's pretty clear what's going on. I mean, you saw them with your own eyes.'

'Yeah,' Hazel agrees.

'What do you mean by *exaggerated*?' Jess asks.

I take a deep breath. 'I think I got a bit carried away when I was telling you about them hooking up outside the supermarket,' I offer.

Hazel frowns. 'As in?'

The word that Kelly has used jumps into my head. *Dilemma*. I'm definitely in one of those. I have to quash the whole idea of Dad and Sandra having an affair, but there are different ways to do that. The best way, I think, is to try to keep the explanation lighthearted. That way, the girls might even think the whole saga was at least entertaining.

I have a flash of the three of them laughing. Slapping me on the back and saying how much I fooled them. I know in my heart that it's not going to happen like that, but it seems like my only chance with them.

'I got the idea off *Acacia Lane*,' I say. They all look bewildered. It's Hazel who gets what I'm saying first.

'You'd already watched it before Friday night,' she says. It's not a question, so I don't answer. But I can see the realisation growing in Edi's eyes and it makes me panic.

'You know,' I say, 'it seemed like a good idea at the time. Like, something to spice things up a bit.'

Hazel tilts her head to the side. Examining me. 'Did it happen at all?' she asks. 'What you told us?'

I don't say anything.

'Hang on,' Jess says. 'Isn't what Olympia said different to what happened on *Acacia Lane*? Because Veronica came out of Juicy Couture, not out of the supermarket and her dad –'

'I think you'll find,' Hazel interrupts, 'that Olympia edited the story to make it more realistic.'

'Olympia, did *any* of it really happen?' It's Edi asking now. She's looking at me as though I'm a complete stranger.

'Not really,' I say. It's small. I wish I could say something to change all this. But what can I say?

'So, it wasn't an *exaggeration*,' Edi says. 'It was a lie.'

Everyone is quiet. Edi hardly ever gets angry. But she is now. I can see it in her eyes, the way her lips are tight, the straight rod of her back.

'Why would you do that?' she says. She doesn't yell, but there's a tone in her voice that tells me she doesn't even want me to answer.

I don't know what to say anyway. My mind is a huge tangle. My mum and dad fighting is tangled with Edi and Hazel getting closer. The lie is tangled with wanting more attention from my friends. I can't find an end anywhere, to shake loose one of the problems so I can look at it by itself.

'We nearly told your mum,' Hazel says. 'Think about what might have happened then.' Her words fly about in the wind.

'If you lied about something that big,' Jess says, 'how can we trust you with other stuff?'

I shrug. I can't think of anything. My legs dangle over the chair, swaying.

'That's it, Jess,' Edi says. Then she turns to me. 'How can we ever know if you're telling the truth? God, you could have made Alec up for all we know.'

Jess shakes her head. 'Actually, come to think of it, I saw Olympia at the skate park. She was by herself.'

Edi and Hazel shake their heads.

'Leo has never heard of a graffiti artist named Alec,' Hazel says.

'I didn't make him up,' I say. I really want them to understand that, at least. But the girls look like they don't believe me.

'Okay, then,' Edi says. 'You said you're going to meet him at the skate park every Saturday. How about we come along and meet him this weekend?'

'He's not going to be there this Saturday.' I sound like a kitten mewing.

'Yeah, right,' Hazel says. 'That figures.'

They all get up out of their seats. They walk out via the side gate. Only Jess looks back.

V

'Limps, what's going on? You've been out here for ages. It's really cold! Dinner's nearly ready.' Mum stands at the back door, her cardigan pulled tight around her.

I get up. I walk inside, with Cricket at my heels. My only friend.

'Olympia, what's wrong?' Mum asks.

I pass her at the door, squeezing through the gap.

'Nothing,' I say. Then I go straight to my room.

'Everything,' I tell Cricket.

I've never been so grateful for sleep, and this is the kindest sort. There are no dreams, no reminders. Just a peaceful nothing. I sleep right through until Mum wakes me for school.

I tell her I'm sick. She lets me stay home. And again, I sleep.

It's mid-morning before I start tossing and turning. There's no sleep left in me, though I *will* it to come again. I want to keep my brain switched off. Because it's there, of course. What happened yesterday is there. I just refuse to consider it. Instead, I reach for my sketchbook.

It's good, losing myself in the portrait of Nick. I've never drawn anyone with this level of detail. My pencil is driven by feeling and instinct rather than thought. I know how I'm going to draw Nick. It's as though I don't have a choice.

I work on the drawing for hours. Finally, I stick it on my wall. I take a step backwards and stare at it.

It's the best thing I've ever created. It's Nick, all excited, his hands pumping in front of him. He's putting weight on his left foot, which makes it look like he's launching himself into the picture, the way he always seems ready to launch into life.

It's Nick. The real Nick. As he is.

V

Mum comes into my bedroom after work. I've been here all day.

'How are you feeling, Olympia?' she asks, sitting on my bed.

'Sick,' I say. 'I think I'll need tomorrow off as well.' I don't want to go to school ever again.

'What kind of sick?' Mum asks. She puts a hand on my forehead, and takes it away without commenting on my lack of fever.

'*Very* sick,' I say with a sigh. 'Please don't make me go.'

Mum fluffs up a pillow and rests it against the head-board of my bed. I move over so she can fit. Cricket slides down the doona between us.

'Something happened yesterday, didn't it, Limps?' she says. 'Did you have a fight with one of the girls? Do you want to tell me what happened?' she asks.

I shake my head. There's no way on earth I want to tell Mum what happened.

It doesn't matter anyway. Like Kelly told me, I can't unsay what I've said to them. My friends just aren't my friends anymore.

Mum turns towards me, propping her head up in her hand.

'Sweetheart, you don't have to tell me if you don't want to. I get that some things are private – just between you and whoever you have a problem with. But you can't run away either. You can't lie here in bed for the rest of your life, because pretty soon you'll realise it doesn't work. That you can't run away from yourself. You have to confront the issue, Limps, whatever it is.'

She sounds like she's reading from one of her stupid self-help books. It's so annoying.

'Why?' I say. 'That's what Dad does.'

Mum blows out a breath. 'You're right. That *is* what your father does. I think it's a sign of his emotional immaturity. When things get tough, when there's a problem or an argument or too much responsibility, he grabs a beer. Or he goes to Aunty Kate's. In some ways, I think, because we got together so young, he hasn't really *grown*. But it's wrong. It doesn't solve anything.'

She breathes in again and I know, I just *know*, she's going to keep complaining about Dad. And I. Don't. Want. To. Hear. It.

'See?' I say, and now it just blurts out of me. 'You do it too. Only you always run to *me*, Mum, and dump all this stuff on me about Dad that I shouldn't even know! Stuff that should be between you and *him*. Maybe that's a sign of emotional immaturity too?'

Mum doesn't say anything. She's probably thinking of a hundred ways to crack it with me.

When she does speak, though, her voice is surprisingly gentle.

'You're right about that too, Olympia,' she says. 'Maybe it's time we all looked at ourselves. It's not like we can escape who we are, but at least we can try to figure it out. I guess ...' She clears her throat. 'I guess because I had you so young, in some ways I treat you as a friend. But you're my daughter.' Mum bites her bottom lip, which has started to wobble.

'Mum,' I say, and all the anger has flown out of me. I think of the message I've been drafting with Kelly and I'm glad I've been doing it. It helps. But I don't need that piece of paper at the moment. I know what I want to say.

'I love that we're friends. I wouldn't change that for anything. I just need you and Dad to know that when you fight in front of me, I feel like you guys don't *see* me, like you don't even know I'm there. You don't realise how much it upsets me. It makes me feel like Dad's going to leave again and our family is going to break up forever. And I do want you to tell me stuff – just not the stuff you tell me about Dad. Because when you do that, it's like I'm supposed to take sides. Which I can't do. It pulls me apart.'

'Limps,' Mum says, 'I get it. Honestly I do. And I'm going to talk to Jim about it. Privately. I promise.' She pulls me into her and gives me a hug. It feels good.

'School tomorrow, Limps,' she says after the hug. Her voice is back to normal. I know there's no point arguing. She's my friend, but this is the *mum* side. 'But what did you do all day today?'

I get out of bed and point at the portrait of Nick. Mum gets up too, and looks at it for ages.

'My talented girl,' she says eventually. 'My smart, talented daughter. You'll figure out how to get through the stuff with your friends, whatever it is.'

I shrug. It's nice to hear Mum say that. And at least I've finally been able to tell her how I feel when she and Dad fight. Now I just need to work out how to talk to my friends.

Thirteen

School feels different on Wednesday. I walk in the front gates as though I'm a new girl, walking in for the first time. Like I have an 'L' on my forehead. A girl who doesn't have any friends.

The breezeway seems to go forever today. I wind through groups of people who are pausing to chat. People who have friends to chat with.

I'm relieved, at least, that the gang isn't at the lockers. In class, I sit at a table by myself and just keep my head down, working really hard. I make sure I don't even look their way, though I think I can feel their eyes boring into me at times. I don't know how I'm supposed to act with them anymore.

At recess, I walk down towards our normal hangout, the slope above the basketball courts. I watch them from a distance. Edi is standing up, her hand shading her forehead in what looks like a salute. I know exactly what that means. She's trying to get a glimpse of Archie on the soccer fields beyond the basketball court. I also know that Archie will come up to the slope to see Edi about five minutes before the bell goes, because that's what they've organised as a compromise.

Hazel is propped up on her elbow on the grass, talking to Leo. Jess is sitting cross-legged beside Hazel. Chester has his arm around her shoulder. His hand is dangling, and I watch as Jess lifts her hand awkwardly, grabs Chester's and moves it to the side. I know exactly why she's doing that too. Jess is trying her best to avoid Chester's hand randomly touching her boob.

Suddenly, Jess turns and looks my way. She extracts her hand from Chester's and waves. I guess, out of our gang,

Jess is the one I haven't taken seriously. The one I don't think about that often. She never seemed to have an edge, I guess. But she's so kind. And, right now, her kindness gives me hope that I haven't lost all my friends.

Now I see Edi and Hazel looking to see who Jess is waving at. Me. It's awful, how they both look away.

I put my head down and walk back up the breezeway alone.

V

At lunchtime, I don't even go down to the slope. Instead, I walk in the exact opposite direction, back towards the school gate. Erin, Briana and Phoebe are sitting at the bench. George is there too, talking with Erin. I wander over, trying to look casual. Trying to look like I'm just checking things out.

When Erin sees me, she beckons me over and makes room beside her on the bench for me. I don't even care that she and George are yakking on about some lame computer game they're both into.

At least it's somewhere to be.

V

I'm glad when the bell goes. This has been one of the longest days of my life, and it's not even over yet.

I rush to the lockers so I can pick up my portrait of Nick before anyone else gets there. I'm the first person in the art room.

I put the portrait facedown on the table in front of me. I'm a bit nervous about showing it to Nick, but I want him to be the first to see it. If he hates it, I won't show anyone else. I'll leave it up to him.

It's not long before the rest of the class turns up. Anya sits next to me and Myra starts setting up some art gear at the front of the room. I notice she has some spraycans and my heart does a little skip as I think of Alec. Who my friends think I've made up.

When Nick arrives, he walks straight over to me. 'Did you do it, Olympia?' he asks excitedly. 'Did you draw a picture of me?'

I nod, one hand on the facedown portrait. I put my other hand up. 'Myra,' I say. 'Do you mind if I go outside with

Nick for a moment to show him something I've drawn?'

Myra nods. 'Okay,' she says, 'as long as you stay right outside, on the steps.'

Nick follows me out of the art room. I sit on a step with the portrait still facedown on my lap. I pat a space beside me and Nick sits down. Then, I turn over the picture.

He looks at it for a moment. 'You didn't make me into the Incredible Hulk,' he says loudly. His forehead is creased in confusion, and he's sitting very still, for Nick.

I've blown it. I've really blown it.

Nick holds out both hands and I put the portrait in them. 'You just drew me, how I actually look,' he says.

'Yeah,' I say.

'But why?' he asks.

I take a deep breath and sigh. It's hard to explain why I wanted to draw him as he is. Of course he's interested to see what he might look like all huge and green and ready to take on the world. But, in a way, that's what I've been doing with myself. Lying to make myself seem somehow bigger, more exciting than I really am. And that hasn't worked *at all*.

'Why didn't you want to draw me as the Incredible Hulk?' Nick asks, but his voice is softer this time. He's staring at the picture in his hands like he's mesmerised.

'Because you're you, Nick,' I say slowly. 'I wanted to capture *you*.'

Nick holds the picture out in front of both of us.

'I like it,' he says finally. 'I look interesting.'

As soon as he says that, I feel better. I've spent half my life thinking about how I can change myself into someone else – with better hair, teeth, legs, clothes. The list pretty much goes on forever. And it's not only the physical stuff.

Kelly was right that I feel like I have to work hard to keep my position in the cool group. And that's another way of trying to be someone else – someone my friends will think is more interesting than plain old Olympia.

The weirdest thing, though, is that it's the people I haven't even *tried* to impress who seem to like me the most. Nick looks very happy with me at the moment. And I'm pretty sure Alec likes me too. It's just there, in the way we get along, in the way he's asked to keep meeting up.

Maybe it's time I stopped trying to turn myself into

something bigger, better, more exciting. Maybe I should just let myself be me.

'This must've taken a long time to draw,' Nick says, interrupting my thoughts. 'Maybe even four hours.'

In fact it took almost double that, but I just nod.

'Can I keep it?' he asks.

I scratch my head. This is the best thing I've ever drawn, and it did take me ages. Part of me doesn't want to give it away. But then I realise it's Nick who should own this picture. The way he owns himself.

'Yep, sure,' I say.

'Thanks, Olympia,' Nick says. 'You're really nice.'

And, right now, I *do* feel nice. Like I've done the right thing for a change.

'Let's show *everyone*,' says Nick.

I follow him back into the classroom. Within seconds, he's showing it around. Nick Bradbury, as he really is.

I wonder if it's too late for me to do that.

Fourteen

Dad doesn't cook very often, but tonight he's made spaghetti carbonara. The three of us sit at the table.

'So, that was a mysterious illness you had yesterday,' Dad says to me. 'It just came and went, didn't it?'

'Oh well, everyone needs a day off sometimes, Jim. A mental health day,' Mum says.

'I'll mention that to my boss,' Dad says.

As soon as he says that, I get a sinking feeling that they're going to fight again. But something else happens.

Dad looks over at Mum. She raises her eyebrows, as

though she's prompting him to think twice before he goes on. He looks back at me.

'I'm glad you're feeling better,' he says. He looks me right in the eyes, and I think I know what's going on. Mum has told him how I feel when they fight, so he's making sure I don't feel ignored. It's a bit awkward, but it's something.

Finally, he looks back at Mum, and a small smile passes between them. As though they're a little bit proud of themselves for not letting this turn into an argument. Not in front of me anyway.

And I know it's weird for me to think it, since I'm the kid, but I'm proud of them too.

V

I'm sitting on my bed. I've had my phone in my hand for ages, but I haven't done it yet.

It's a risk. The girls might not want anything to do with me anymore. But I have to give it a go.

I run through it in my mind, trying to practise what I'm going to say, like Kelly's taught me.

I want to suggest a meeting before school tomorrow. Even if it goes really badly, at least I'll know. I don't want to go through another day like today, in limbo land.

I don't want it to be at Edi's caravan, or in the drama room. There have been loads of meetings between us in both those places. I really want to try somewhere new, because that's what I'm hoping for. A fresh start.

Finally, I type in the text.

Any chance of meeting at the skate park 8 am tomoz? I know it's early, but I want to explain. O.

I wait. Stare at the screen.

Jess's text comes back first. Like she doesn't even need to consider it.

See u there x

If I'm ever allowed back in the group, I'm going to be different with Jess. She's really special.

Finally, the phone beeps with two more messages.

Ok

K

They're not exactly the warmest texts I've ever received. But at least they're going to give me a go.

V

I make sure I arrive at the skate park first. There are only a few skaters doing manoeuvres on the ramp. No-one we know, luckily.

Edi, Hazel and Jess all arrive together. When I see them, they're walking really slowly. I'm pretty sure that Hazel and Edi are setting the pace, because Jess keeps having to wait for them. It's as though they're not convinced they should be here. Then Jess ups the pace and walks straight over to the bench where I'm sitting. She throws her schoolbag on the table and takes a seat next to me.

'Hey, Limps, how's it going? It's a much nicer day than yesterday, but Tuesday was really crap. You were lucky you were away. It was pouring, and we all begged Miss Kearns to do an inside game, but she was all, "Come on, it's only spitting," and Leni's all like, "If you run you can hardly feel the rain," and then we spent the whole period on the oval and everyone was soaked. You should see Anya's hair when it's wet. It's full-on curly. Adam looked like a drowned rat ...' Jess shakes her head and smiles. She seems to remember why she started talking about Tuesday in the first place, just as Hazel and Edi get to us. 'So, why were you away?' Jess asks.

Hazel sits on the other side of the table, but Edi stays standing up, as though she wants to have the option of getting away fast. I have an urge to say I was sick, but I stop myself. If I'm ever going to fix things, I need to start with the truth.

I clear my throat. It's one thing finding the right words when you're alone in your bedroom, but it's completely another when you have to share them. 'I was kind of depressed,' I say. 'Because I've been an idiot.'

I silently will Edi to sit down with us. It seems to work. She slides into the bench seat next to Hazel. I take a deep breath. Here goes.

'My parents had an argument last Sunday night, and I was still upset the next day at school, you know, when we had maths and PE.' I start slowly, looking down at the table. I try to ease myself into this. 'It was pretty much one of their normal arguments.'

I risk a quick glance across the table. Hazel and Edi are

listening, but Hazel is frowning. Edi raises her eyebrows, like she's exasperated. They've heard this all before, of course. They're waiting for more. I look down again.

'The thing is, even though it's normal for them to fight, I never get used to it. That night, it felt worse than usual.' I put my head in my hands, and then pull them down again. If I'm going to do this, I can't hide away. I lift my head and direct the next bit at Edi. 'I saw the *Sunday Style Snapshot* where you said you were shopping with Hazel, and it felt ... it just felt like you guys were getting really close and I ...' I heave out a sigh. This is tough. 'I was jealous, I guess.'

'Olympia,' Edi says. Her voice is hard. 'You really have to stop trying to control everything. It's kind of suffocating.' She looks like she's considering whether to say something else. I wait. 'You can't own people, Olympia.'

It hits hard, like a thump in my chest. I'm *not* Edi's one and only best friend. And the harder I've tried to make that true, the more I seem to have pushed her away.

'Olympia, you have to let people do whatever they want to do with whoever they want to do it with. I can't ...

It should be okay for any of us to hang out without having to feel bad about it. Like, we're *all* supposed to be friends.'

It's true, what she's said. I know I've been kind of crazy about wanting to be closest to Edi. But Hazel and Jess are my friends too. I suppose I haven't made it easy.

'You're a really good friend,' Edi says and now her voice is softer, as though she's got out at least one of her main frustrations. 'You're *so* loyal when I have a problem. I want to be loyal right back to you. But it stresses me out when you're upset about not being included in *everything*. Can you please try not to worry about that stuff so much?'

At least Edi has told me I'm smart and loyal. The fact that she's asked me to try seems to suggest she's thinking of giving me a second chance.

I nod. 'I'll try,' I say.

'What does all this have to do with the story you made up about your dad and Sandra?' Hazel asks. As usual, she's the one getting all practical and logical and trying to put the puzzle pieces together. But today, I don't mind. Today, I want to try to get the full picture of me and our group, even if it hurts.

I think of the portrait I gave Nick, of how he ended up liking it. It was true to him. It gives me strength to tell my own truth.

'It was kind of a combination of things,' I say. 'My parents were arguing, and I felt like I was losing you, Edi. Like you didn't find me as interesting as Hazel now that she has a boyfriend and ...'

'Hey, whoa there,' Jess interrupts. 'What am I? Chopped liver?'

'No, I was just about to say that you also have a boyfriend,' I begin, but there's something about Jess, a lightness, that sort of infiltrates our mood. When I look up at Edi and Hazel, they're both biting their lips, trying not to smile.

'It was yuck,' I continue. 'But such *ordinary* yuck. Then I saw that episode of *Acacia Lane* and even though Dad wasn't having an affair, the way he and Mum argue sometimes *feels* just as upsetting to me. It had been building up. Every night with them, even if things were fine, I was waiting for something to go wrong. Then, waiting again for Mum to come and dump it all on me.' I pause and look around the table. I can tell my friends are listening to me. *Seeing* me. 'I know it was dumb, but I used the story from *Acacia Lane* because I thought it might make you guys understand how I felt. I'm really sorry. It was a stupid lie.'

Edi sighs. 'It *was* stupid, Limps,' she says. She hasn't called me that for days.

'But I kind of get it now,' Hazel adds. 'It must be awful when your parents fight. Your mum should stop talking to you about your dad, too.'

'You've got to tell her,' Edi says.

'Actually, I did tell her,' I say. 'I've been seeing Kelly Alisi, and she helped me to figure out what to say. And so far, it's making things better.'

'That's good, Limps,' Edi says softly. She grabs my hand over the table. 'But no more lies, hey? Or we won't know when to believe you.'

I get the feeling that she still thinks I've been lying about Alec. That I've made him up. But I don't feel like protesting about that right now. Right now, it's enough if we can all just be friends again. Even if that means letting go of the idea that Edi is *my* best friend and mine only.

'Well, you can lie about *small* things,' Jess says. 'Like, if you really hate someone's clothes, then you shouldn't actually tell them exactly ...'

Hazel holds her hand up in the familiar stop sign. I feel the beginnings of a smile creep onto my face.

V

It's time to go to school. We get up from the bench. Hazel does a detour to check out Leo's graffiti on the wall.

'Hey, over here,' she calls. We backtrack over to the graffiti wall.

'Check this out,' Hazel says, pointing. There's a lot of graffiti up there. It's a while before I see it, next to Alec's picture of Barney. It's Cricket! I know as soon as I see it. He's captured the way she often has one ear up and one down. She's leaping in the air, and under her is a caption: *You make my heart leap!*

He's done it just for me. Without me even trying, without me being somebody other than who I really am. Which makes it feel even more like a gift.

'Looks like there's a new graffiti artist around here,' Hazel says.

They all look at me, grinning. We link arms. The four of us. And we're still linking arms when we walk into the school gates. Together.

GIRL V THE WORLD

I Heart You, Archie de Souza

Edi lives a weird double life. At school it seems like everyone loves her, but at home her parents barely notice she exists – except when her marks aren't good enough.

So when Edi hooks up with her crush Archie, she can hardly believe her luck. Archie is super cute, and his family are warm and welcoming. Edi wants to spend every waking minute with Archie, even if it means letting her friends and schoolwork slide. But does Archie feel the same way?

How To Boost Your Profile

Anya needs some serious cheering up. She's been dumped by a nerd, her parents are splitting up, and her mum's idea of a first bra is going to ruin her life!

But then Anya discovers a way to get what she wants. Yes, it's against the rules, but surely she bend them, just to give herself a boost? It's not like she's hurting anyone ....

Waiting For It

When the boys at school put up a list of the hottest girls in her year, Hazel is ranked halfway down. It figures. Even on something as stupid as a hot list, Hazel is stuck in the middle.

She's sick of being *nearly-but-not-quite* grown-up, *kind-of* popular, *almost* good-looking. And she's sick of waiting for things to change. It's time to take matters into her own hands!

It's Not Me, It's You

Erin doesn't know exactly *when* it happened, but it happened. Boys started being boyfriends. Girls started wearing make-up to school. And her big sister started keeping secrets about her love-life.

It seems like everyone is changing around Erin, and yet she's still the same. She's fine doing her own thing, but she never thought she'd be deliberately left out. How can Erin grow up and just be herself?

Things I Don't Know

Leni doesn't understand her friends or family at all. Why does Anya want to start a dumb kissing competition? Why won't her grandmother quit smoking? And why is her athletics buddy Adam acting like a big weirdo around her?

The Leni meets Jo ... the new girl at school. She's cool and fun, and totally on Leni's wavelength. But as their friendship grows, Leni finds she has questions about Jo too. Or maybe they are questions about herself. Whatever it is, she doesn't know the answers!